"You're cheating."

There was a tremor in Alex's voice as if he was hanging on to control by a very slender thread.

"What?" *What was he talking about?* Natalie was stunned by the ferocity of his unexpected attack. Putting down the phone, she watched as Alex angrily got out of the rumpled bed. *Where was her passionate and tender lover of only moments ago?*

"You had me fooled. Completely." His tone was even as he hurriedly dressed. Natalie pulled her robe more closely around her with trembling fingers. He turned hard and accusing eyes on her, daring her to contradict him. "Did you think I'd whisper the answers in my sleep?"

All of Natalie's hopes, her dreams that Alex could love her, collapsed like a house of cards. "No, Alex, you don't understand—"

"Don't I?" He laughed bitterly. "Isn't this what you planned all along? That I'd lead you to the treasure if you slept with me?"

Emma Jane Spenser is a Temptation success story! Her very first book, *A Novel Approach*, won the *Romantic Times* Reviewer's Choice Award for the Best Temptation. *Two Can Play*, her third sexy and funny Temptation novel, features an intricate puzzle and a cast of eccentric characters in a romp through merry old England—home to Emma Jane as her husband finished his doctorate at Oxford.

Currently, Emma Jane, her husband and their son live in beautiful California, where she continues to weave her highly imaginative stories. Don't miss *Detente*— the end of a cold war between a very passionate but unlikely couple—available in February 1991.

Books by Emma Jane Spenser

HARLEQUIN TEMPTATION
248–A NOVEL APPROACH
273–THAT HOLIDAY FEELING

EC A+

Two Can Play

EMMA JANE SPENSER

Harlequin Books

TORONTO • NEW YORK • LONDON
AMSTERDAM • PARIS • SYDNEY • HAMBURG
STOCKHOLM • ATHENS • TOKYO • MILAN

For Grace

Published December 1990

ISBN 0-373-25427-X

TWO CAN PLAY

Prologue

BEADS OF SWEAT gathered on his forehead and upper lip as Stanhope listened to the words that spelled his ruin. It was over now, before it had really begun. Straining to keep his voice even, he thanked the caller for keeping him informed and hung up the telephone.

It was that new vice president's fault. No one else had even considered the need for a test, but now they were all sold on the idea. All they needed was a professional who could solve the puzzle.

He had to do something to stop it.

For a moment Stanhope wished he'd never heard of the treasure hunt story... or stolen the prize.

Dragging unsteady fingers through his hair, he considered the options. It was too late to change their minds. But he couldn't take the chance that the person they hired would somehow solve the puzzle, because the treasure was no longer there. He needed more time—time to pin the blame onto someone else. Failing that, he'd need to get away.

A sudden calm overtook him, the barest suggestion of a smile lifted the corners of his mouth as the solution became clear.

He would ensure the sleuth didn't solve the puzzle—no matter what.

1

"YES, DEAR. I've already looked in the usual places. It's not there."

Natalie wedged the telephone between her shoulder and ear as she struggled to pull on her other shoe. The last time she'd gone jogging in these shoes, her neighbor, old Mr. Langdon, had unleashed a torrent of water directly in her path. Well, perhaps torrent was a bit of an exaggeration. Generously Natalie reduced her description to cascade. Either way, it wasn't as if he'd done it on purpose. Just as she didn't consider the old man crazy to water his shrubs in the early, Boston spring, Mr. Langdon had never suggested that running in the snow or rain was more than mildly eccentric. They had a relationship built upon mutual tolerance.

"Have you tried the fruit basket above the refrigerator?" Natalie kept her voice even, her mind considering the possibilities. Abandoning her struggles with the knot, she gave her full attention to Mrs. Wilkins.

"Yes, Natalie," Mrs. Wilkins replied. "The fruit basket is on that list you gave me."

Natalie reeled off another half-dozen possibilities, listening resignedly to the negative answers. Naturally, the elderly woman had looked everywhere. Mrs. Wilkins always looked everywhere. That is, she looked everywhere on the list.

Unfortunately, Natalie had never found Mrs. Wilkins's watch in the same place twice. The list was actually more of a directory of places where she *wouldn't* find it.

Now it was lost. Again. And it was Natalie's job to find it. It was just one of the many tasks she took on as the head of her own investigative firm, Lost & Found, Inc. And while waging a running battle with a perpetually missing wristwatch wasn't perhaps the most difficult job she had ever tackled, it was certainly one of her favorites. More importantly, it provided a contrast to the more dramatic cases she became involved in, lending a sense of balance whenever she felt her nerves stretched to the breaking point.

Natalie looked at the time then said, "I'm on my way home. I'll detour past your place and see what I can do." Changing her route appealed to Natalie. The area around her client's home was flat and quiet, unlike her usual route between home and office, one that was dominated by hills and traffic.

Standing on one foot, Natalie stretched across the desk and punched another button on the telephone console. "Where's that pair of shoes I wore in this morning?" she asked. The knot had temporarily defeated her, and it was her nature to avoid small frustrations whenever possible. She was already planning on stopping at the corner market to buy another pair of laces to replace the ones she was going to cut.

"Gone with the wind." Natalie could picture her secretary's pleased smirk. Liz had been hinting for weeks about tossing out Natalie's favorite pair of running shoes. Just last week Liz had suggested a raise would be in order if she had to look at them drying on the bathroom windowsill much longer. Natalie was convinced that Liz was merely intimidated by their brilliant yellow hue. An ardent supporter of armchair exercise, Liz regarded the shoes as a blatant contradiction to her firm belief that she could stay fit without lifting a finger. If you equated fitness with being slender, Natalie had to concede Liz was winning.

"You mean . . . ?" she asked quietly, already mourning their demise even as she plotted to investigate the neon-green pair she'd spotted in the local sports shop.

"Yup. Six feet under. Lost in space. Disappeared without a trace." Knowing Liz could go on forever, Natalie disconnected the intercom with a flick of her finger and settled down in the oversize leather chair to attack the wretched shoe once more. It took five minutes and a pair of tweezers, but finally the shoelace was untied. Collecting a stack of things she would need for her trip to England the next day, that included her field binoculars, American-British Dictionary and her favorite collapsible umbrella, Natalie stopped by her secretary's desk on the way out. Liz calmly added the pile to one of her own, barely managing to stifle a smirk, her boss noted.

"I'll meet you at your place in an hour," Liz called as Natalie headed for the door.

Natalie ignored her. As far as she was concerned, they weren't on speaking terms.

NATALIE NEVER quite understood how she could get so hot and sweaty by running a few miles. It didn't make sense, particularly when everyone she passed was wrapped up tightly against the brisk, March winds. But that didn't make her any less hot and sweaty and generally out of breath, and she was grateful when she finally pushed open the door to her apartment and Liz stuck a tall, frosty glass of water into her hand.

As a peace offering it was a good start.

"Did you find it?"

Natalie drank half the contents of the glass, then nodded.

"Anywhere interesting?" Liz asked.

"In her telephone book," she gasped. "Her personal book. Not the city one."

Natalie went into the kitchen with Liz following, and poured more water into her glass. Another long sip, and she sensed she was on the verge of recovery. She leaned heavily against the sink, trying to convince her legs of that as she tugged at the rubber band to free her hair. Catching her reflection in the mirror that filled the space between cabinet and window, Natalie grimaced at the long, thick mane of auburn hair that was darkened with sweat. Sweat also glistened on her face, her delicate features flushed from her exertion. She looked more like an inverse Christmas tree than a woman, she decided, with her green eyes standing out against the red background of her face. A short Christmas tree, she amended, as she rose on tiptoe to crack open the window. At a little over five feet three inches, such tasks were far from easy, and she had to jump a little before the window came unstuck.

"I'll never understand why you put yourself through this."

For a moment, Natalie wasn't sure whether Liz was referring to the fact that she should have used a footstool or to her exercise regimen. Either way, she decided not to answer. She was still miffed about the shoes.

"It's not because you like it," Liz persisted. "I know you don't."

"You're right," Natalie said, relenting. "I don't like it. I hate it."

"Then why do you bother?"

"Because when I'm done and I can finally breathe again, I'm so glad it's over." Natalie grinned at the bewildered expression on Liz's face.

"I don't believe it."

Natalie broadened her grin, but declined to argue the point.

"Anything you want to tell me about the stuff on the table, besides the fact it probably weighs more than you and me put together?"

Liz ignored the barb, confident that Natalie would need every book, map and brochure that she had painstakingly collected. "Only that while you are in England, you can probably get into a library if you need to. But be careful. A lot of them are only reading, not lending libraries. And some won't let you in at all without special permission."

Natalie nodded, never once questioning how Liz had found out about the libraries and their restrictions. As administrative head of the office, she was expected to know these things—or find them out. While Natalie was the creative genius behind the agency, Liz's role was equally essential. Her dedication to her job freed Natalie to do what she liked best. Find things. But recently Natalie had realized it wasn't enough to pay Liz for a job well-done. When she returned from England, she planned to offer her a full partnership.

Goodness knows, Natalie was certainly ready to share the burden of management. It had been six long years since she'd completed her training and gone out on her own, six years since she'd coaxed Liz into going with her. At first, it had been just the two of them in a second-story walk-up that passed for an office. Their fledgling agency had the name on the door—and not much else. Lost & Found, Inc., had succeeded thanks to lots of hard work and a little luck.

Now, with six full time investigators on staff, they took on everything from lost wills to lost children. Their larger offices were now located on the fifth floor of a modern building in downtown Boston, and an elevator had superseded the long flight of stairs. Liz still managed the office with flair as Natalie and her team of investigators unraveled whatever cases came their way.

Yes, she affirmed silently, it was only right that she offer Liz the partnership. But first, Natalie had a treasure to find in England and as always, Liz was sending her fully prepared. The maps and books would guide her as she sorted through the clues, finding the trail. There was more than her professional honor at stake. True, if she won the game her reputation would be made. But as of yesterday, when she'd learned through Stanhope that the treasure hunt's creator had summarily dismissed her chances as nil, this job had become a personal dare.

Liz pointed to another stack of documents and papers. "Your passport, tickets and hotel reservations. You'll pick up the rental car at Heathrow, and as it's a short drive to the hotel don't worry about what lane you're driving in. Just follow the traffic, and try not to shift with your right hand. You'll either break your arm or put your fist through the window.

"You can leave for the Cotswolds the next morning," Liz continued. "Here are some traveler's checks in pounds, and enough cash to get you started."

Hardly stopping for a breath, Liz listed the remaining papers. "The color proofs of *The Quest* arrived today from Neil Stanhope's office," she said, referring to the book upon which the treasure hunt was based and her contact at Dempsey Press, the publisher.

"Did you get Stanhope's home number in case I need to check in at odd hours?" With a three week time restriction, she needed twenty-four hour access to her contact.

"It's in your notebook, along with an alternate number for his associate."

"Did you get Garrick's address?"

"Also in your notebook." Liz hesitated a moment before adding, "Stanhope was reluctant to give it to you, said something about it being confidential."

"He'd already given me the name," Natalie reminded her.

"You tricked him into telling you—"

"Nevertheless, if I could find out by being a little sneaky, then someone else might just have the same luck," Natalie said. "If Alexander Garrick wants to hide behind the pen name Gregory Lewis, he'll have to do a better job of covering his tracks." But she smiled because she was a little star-struck at the prospect of meeting the famous author.

"Stanhope asked why you wanted it in the first place."

Natalie blew her bangs out of her face. "Garrick is as much a part of this treasure hunt as any other clue we've got. He wrote *The Quest*, and he'll have put a lot of himself into it." A nervous tightening of her stomach muscles reminded Natalie this was the most unusual case her firm had ever tackled. Over the next three weeks, all of her skills would be in constant demand as she followed the threads of logic and luck to solve the puzzle.

"Then that's it. I'm out of here," Liz reached for her purse.

She probably had a date, Natalie decided. "Anybody I know?"

"It's Darrin. We're going to a revival of Frank Capra's *Lost Horizon*. Don't look so surprised," Liz chided her friend. "You knew it had to happen sooner or later."

"I did?" Shaking her head slowly, Natalie reviewed what she knew about Darrin. Not only had Liz taken extreme caution over the past several months to avoid this particular member of the male species, she had been eloquent in her disparagement of this onetime boyfriend. Spineless, ineffective and wishy-washy were just a few of the adjectives Liz had used. And, according to her latest soliloquy on the hapless accountant, he had even fewer redeeming qualities than Natalie's abhorrent running shoes.

Liz nodded, misinterpreting Natalie's stunned expression. "You're shocked it took so long. So am I. But I guess some things just take longer than others. And Darrin's mom was a tougher nut to crack than I had first thought."

Darrin's mom? Natalie was lost, but nodded encouragingly.

"Don't worry about anything while you're gone." Liz ordered as she charged out the door.

Natalie stared at the open doorway, replaying the disjointed conversation, trying to focus on the image of Liz and Darrin together.

When she couldn't quite picture that, Natalie returned to her unusual assignment. Nearly a week earlier, Natalie had been approached by a senior member of the New York publishing firm, Dempsey Press. Mr. Brooks had learned of Natalie's unique investigative

agency in the wake of the tremendous publicity over
her last case which involved locating a Meissen figu-
rine, one of a pair dating back to the early 19th century. After months of tracing past owners and
unraveling its long and colorful history—the set had
been divided nearly 130 years earlier—she'd finally
discovered it on a shelf in a young girl's bedroom, a
knickknack sharing space with a glass poodle and a
stuffed miniature pony. Her client, a local museum, had
only been too delighted to establish a college fund for
the little girl, and Natalie had the good fortune of earn-
ing a fat fee along with the accompanying publicity.

Mr. Brooks had told her about their upcoming treasure hunt book, *The Quest*. Readers were to follow the
clues to a hidden prize, a treasure valued somewhere in
excess of $100,000. She'd asked what the prize was but
that too was a secret because knowing what it was
might point to where it was hidden. Or it might not,
he'd added with a sly smile.

Mr. Brooks had then related their dilemma. Now,
just when they were ready to go to print, a new vice
president had decided *The Quest* had to be tested to
make sure the puzzle was neither too easy nor too hard.
With Natalie's expertise in tracking down lost or hidden objects, she was the perfect choice for the job, he'd
said.

But in order to have the book in the stores before
Christmas, printing had to begin as soon as possible. If
she couldn't find the treasure in three weeks, changes
would have to be made to the book and publication
would be postponed.

Three weeks wasn't a lot of time, and they didn't want
her wasting precious hours figuring out the location
clues. One of their British editors had deciphered those

for her. While the book would be marketed primarily in the United States, the hunt for the treasure was based in the United Kingdom.

Natalie was elated and a little intimidated. For the next three weeks she would match wits with a master in the art of intrigue, fantasy and deception. Alexander Garrick, author of topical crime thrillers and murder mystery writer, had branched out into puzzle books under the alias of Gregory Lewis. This fascinating tidbit from the publishers was more than enough to convince Natalie that her first stop had to be Alexander Garrick's home. If nothing else, she would learn a little about the man and if she was lucky, get an indication of how his mind worked. That might be the most important clue of all.

It was up to Natalie to decipher the clues and figure out where they might lead her. Then, during daily telephone consultations with Stanhope, she would present the options and receive his feedback. If none of the directions she proposed was correct, he would simply tell her to try again. This would save her weeks of following false trails. And, considering her three-week limit, she needed all the positive guidance she could get!

The only real obstruction she faced was Alexander Garrick. According to Stanhope, he was not pleased to have this test thrown in at the last possible moment. Garrick had even stated that Natalie hadn't a hope in hell of deciphering the puzzle in only three weeks.

Natalie realized that Stanhope's version of his conversation was heavily edited. Obviously the author was a man to be avoided—so she'd be in and out of his life before he knew who she was.

2

STANHOPE HAD THOUGHT it couldn't get worse. He was wrong.

Not only was the Tracy woman on her way to England, she intended to see Garrick. And there was no way to stop her, not without drawing attention to himself.

At least, not from New York.

If he was in England he could keep an eye on her. He could follow her around, make sure she didn't move too quickly.

But he couldn't leave New York. It had taken some fancy footwork to get the boss to let him supervise the treasure hunt, and it would raise too many questions if he suddenly left now. Besides, as long as he was her sole contact, he could control her. At the very least, he'd always know where she was.

He needed help and he knew the exact man for the job—Ned Murdoch. This was different from their first joint venture, but Stanhope thought the seedy little man just might enjoy his new assignment.

Too much was at stake—for both of them—to risk letting Natalie Tracy stumble upon their secret.

NATALIE SNUGGLED DEEPER into the warmth of her sheepskin coat, grateful for the impulse that had caused her to bring it along. Added to the wool slacks, a double layer of sweaters and knee-high, leather boots, she just might survive the next ten minutes or so. Anything beyond that was pure fantasy.

She'd been standing on the hill overlooking the house for hours, waiting for the elusive Alexander Garrick to show himself. This was Natalie's last resort in her search for information about the famous author, but with the cold wind snapping at the exposed bits of her face, she questioned whether the tactic was worth the trouble.

Lifting the binoculars, she focused on the front door for the umpteenth time. Still nothing. With a sigh of disgust, Natalie let the glasses fall and leaned against the slender birch at her back. "He can't stay in there forever," she muttered, refusing to acknowledge the possibility that he wasn't home. Fate wouldn't be so cruel, she silently prayed. The grocer's wife had been quite explicit that Alexander Garrick was not only in town, but holed up in his house, writing another one of those cracking-good spy stories.

That bit of information was the only luck Natalie had had all day. Not that the woman had been any more forthcoming than the rest of the villagers. But by sheer chance, Natalie had entered the small corner shop as the woman was talking on the telephone, discussing the order for supplies she'd received from "that nice Mr. Garrick."

It had taken the better part of the afternoon to stumble upon that tidbit of information. Until then, absolutely no one in the village of Foxfoot had had anything to say about the elusive novelist—good, bad or indifferent. At first, Natalie had tried to strike up conversations with the locals, satisfying a sincere interest in the area before subtly diverting the talk to the famous author.

Her clever tactics hadn't worked. To be sure, she'd been overwhelmed with information about the local sights and wonders. But everyone had shut up tighter than a clam whenever she redirected the conversation to Alexander Garrick. Each and every one of the villagers with whom she had spoken had wished her an agreeable visit, then removed themselves from her presence and her questions.

Mr. Garrick seemed to be a member of a protected species, shielded against the outside world in this tiny, Cotswold village. Natalie wondered briefly what he had done to deserve such loyalty, then lifted the glasses once more. The light was getting so bad that even if he did appear, it would be nearly impossible to recognize him. Another few minutes and she'd have to resort to Plan B.

Natalie wasn't even sure what Plan A had comprised. Because of the total lack of cooperation from the inhabitants of Foxfoot, she had decided upon a frontal assault. But she couldn't march up to the front door and demand entry. First of all, he most likely had a housekeeper—Natalie figured the reaction of the villagers was probably typical of everyone else who came into contact with the man. She'd never make it inside.

Her approach from now on had to be more subtle. With only vague scenarios in mind, she had hung her binoculars around her neck and proceeded to tramp across the Cotswold fields, bounded by their low, stone walls, until she was within sight of his home. Now she waited, hoping he'd come out and...feed the sheep, or something. Barring that, maybe he'd come out for a walk. What she would do then was anyone's guess. Natalie worked best when improvising.

She shook her head impatiently. He wasn't coming out, she couldn't get in. And it was growing colder. And darker. While admitting defeat wasn't easy, it was the next, logical step. But that meant she'd go on to Oxford without any concrete information about the author, unless you counted reclusiveness as an important trait. Natalie didn't think so and raised the glasses once more. She didn't even seriously believe Plan B would work. Oh, she'd give it a try. But her chances of getting her hands on his unlisted number were about as good as getting any more information from the people in the village.

It was time to move, count this as one day wasted and press on with the hunt. She had one more day of scheduled rest before the official start of the hunt, and there was no sense in spending it here. Maybe she would leave for Oxford the next morning. But she was unhappy about leaving loose ends, particularly so early in the game.

Perhaps it was for the best, Natalie reasoned. Still she would have enjoyed meeting the man behind the thrillers. She liked his work, particularly his characters. His style was honest, sometimes brutally so. There was no room in his books for macho spies and beguiling Mata Haris.

But there was another, more personal reason for her disappointment. Alexander Garrick had an incredibly interesting face. Interesting—even intriguing. The black-and-white photograph on the dust jackets of his books was grainy and somewhat indistinct, but Natalie had been absorbed by the image. Taken separately, the features were nothing special, not if you focused on the light-colored hair, the dark eyes, or even the usual lines and creases one would expect from a man who had lived for thirty-six years. But there was something else. . . .

With a final glance through the lenses, Natalie growled her disgust and began to turn away.

"Boo."

"Ayy!" Natalie jumped and fell to her knees, her limbs reduced to quivering nerves and goose bumps. The binoculars swung in a near-perfect circle around her neck, the strap tightening around her throat. Boo? she wondered as her scattered wits began to return. Simple, but effective.

She studied the thick wool slacks that probably sheltered knees and calves and thighs. With only inches between her nose and his legs, it was impossible to see the face of her tormentor. Well, not impossible, but if she lifted her chin, there was a distinct possibility she'd lose her balance again. That didn't appeal to her already wounded sense of decorum. Natalie remained in a crouching position, gathering her wits as her leg muscles regained their ability to support her weight.

It didn't occur to her to be frightened. How could she be scared of a man who said boo? And it was certainly a man. Starting with the deep, almost gravelly pitch of his voice—for a clever investigator, even single syllables are adequate for gender identification—and ending with the long, sturdy legs in front of her face, Natalie knew she'd been surprised by a male of the species.

And she had a sneaking suspicion she knew which male it was. Plan A was rolling right along, if just a little out of control.

"Ayy?" He spoke again, and Natalie, forgetting her resolve, snapped her head back to look at the mouth that mimicked her. The law of gravity did precisely what it had threatened and pulled her down, to land gracelessly, with a thud and a crack, on her back among the stones and frozen mulch that covered the ground. The field glasses now lodged awkwardly between her shoulder blades.

To make matters worse, she'd had a split-second glimpse of the face from the dust jacket. It wasn't interesting. It was absorbing. Compelling. Incredibly sensuous.

"Ouch!" she yelped in a delayed reaction to the sharp pebbles that were digging into her backside, squeezing her eyes shut against the temptation to sneak another look at his face. "Dang it, anyway!" she swore, wincing as she raised a gloved hand to free the binoculars, before they were permanently molded into the contours of her back. She then shifted slightly and began to rub her head.

"Dang it?" he repeated. Natalie thought she heard a chuckle, but it was camouflaged by the crunch of shoes on rock as he knelt beside her. Gentle hands brushed her own aside before probing through her hair, delicately searching for cuts and bumps. Natalie wondered if he could feel her wounded pride. With almost everything above her neck frozen, she couldn't feel a thing except the warming caress of his fingers. It was impossible to plan her next move when all conscious thought was centered on the hands that were bringing warmth and comfort to her head, so Natalie simply gave up and wallowed in the exquisite sensation. She would worry about Plan A later.

"Open your eyes." The firm demand was somehow gentled by the husky timbre of his voice. Natalie was lulled into a feeling of absolute security and trust.

She had no intention of returning to the real world, especially when she was enjoying the best—and only—head massage she'd ever had outside a hair salon. Besides, if she opened her eyes she'd remember she should be angry with him for scaring her nearly half to death, and would very likely start an argument. That would mean she'd have to look at the man's face again and she wasn't strong enough to resist its mysterious pull. Not yet. The finger that traced her brow, the line of her jaw and the contour of her ear was already as familiar as her oldest friend—and as exciting as a midsummer thunderstorm.

"You're not hurt," the voice insisted with absolute confidence, cradling her head in one hand as the other continued to strike her cheek lightly. "You might talk a little oddly, but I'm quite sure you're not hurt."

"Talk oddly?" This from a man who said boo? Suddenly indignant, Natalie jackknifed into a sitting position. Or rather she tried to sit up, but the top of her hard head met his firm chin with a resounding *thwack*. Natalie bounced back to rejoin the mulch and pebbles, her head throbbing. But even with bells and whistles in her ears, it was impossible to ignore the stream of expletives that flowed from his lips. He was freely throwing around words that had long ago been eradicated from her own vocabulary, thanks to a stern mother and an unlimited supply of soap. Obviously, Alexander Garrick's mother hadn't used much soap.

Uttering a final epithet, Alexander Garrick straightened to stand beside her. The throbbing in her head was momentarily forgotten as she felt strong hands reach down to grasp her arms and haul her to her feet. The field glasses tried their best to strangle her—again—but an impatient hand slipped the strap from her neck and tossed the offending object aside.

For a moment Natalie was conscious only of the strength of the hands that held her steady. Then she opened her eyes. And stared. Even in anger the attraction was there . . . and it knocked her sideways. She hadn't imagined it. For the first time Natalie was frightened.

Her eyes roamed his face, searching for clues, for words to describe what was happening to her. His features were not much different from those in the photograph, the light-colored hair more of a sandy blonde than she had imagined, the dark eyes a warm shade of brown. Thick brows, maybe a few shades darker than his hair, were drawn together over eyes that studied her curiously in return. Her gaze traveled along the clean-cut lines of a firm jaw and the slight imperfection of a once-broken nose that suggested a streak of stubbornness.

There was nothing remarkable about him. Nothing to explain what she was feeling.

Always practical, never reckless, here she was, standing in the cold, March wind on a hillside in the middle of England, responding to something she couldn't even define. It wasn't what he'd said—most of the words he had used in the last few moments were unrepeatable. It wasn't how he touched her—although the impersonal grasp of his hands on her arms branded her, even through the thick layers of winter clothing she wore.

Was she suffering from a bizarre form of jet lag?

That errant thought brought her back to earth with yet another thud. She shook her head impatiently, as if the movement would dispel her fanciful imaginings.

"What are you looking for?" he murmured as his eyes undertook a leisurely exploration of her face.

"You," she breathed, the cold wind tearing the word from her mouth and throwing it at the man who stood just inches away. "I was looking for you."

"I don't think I understand."

"I believed it would make things easier," she explained patiently, nibbling at her bottom lip as she acknowledged the fallacy in her plan. That had been before she had met him. Now, instead of having a clear concept of what she had to do, Natalie found herself wondering how she'd be able to concentrate at all.

"Make what easier?"

"The game," she replied slowly, disoriented by her inability to dismiss the bewildering sensations overriding every thought.

His eyes registered her confusion, her concern—neither of which made any sense to him. In fact, nothing was making sense, least of all the trembling woman beside him. What game could she be referring to? The villagers had alerted him to the presence of a stranger, eager to meet the man behind the best-selling espionage books.

While he resented the invasion of his privacy, his gaze was drawn to her moist, full lips. She was worrying the bottom one, biting it delicately with perfectly even teeth, her tongue darting out to soothe the hurt. He found himself almost paralyzed by the urge to put his mouth where his eyes were resting, to thrust his tongue between her lips and into the sweet warmth. Shocked by this unbidden desire, he tore his eyes away to watch her eyes. Green, as rich as a pair of emeralds, they were shadowed by heavy lashes. Those eyes were looking for something.

He hoped she found it.

She raised an impatient hand, drawing back the heavy weight of her hair. The deep auburn color shone even in the gathering dusk, and he imagined the flaming highlights that the light of a warm, crackling fire would create. Alex felt his body tighten as he recalled the soft waves that had just moments before clung lovingly to his fingers, enticing him with their silky abundance. He wanted to touch her again, draw the fine strands through his fingers, perhaps tease her delicate brow with their gentle curls. Alex imagined the rich color in exciting contrast to the cream, satin sheets of his bed, spread across his pillow, framing a face that was alive with anticipation.

Stunned, he took a deep breath, aware that his control over his own desires was weakening by the second. But his gaze was suddenly drawn to her ringless hand, reddened by the biting cold and wind. She'd removed her glove, and he was reminded of the rapidly falling night.

Intruder or spy, he would take her into his home. He wanted to hear about the *game* she had referred to. But as his eyes returned to her full, moist lips, he knew the real reason.

She was exciting, intoxicating. He wanted her.

"It's cold. We should go in."

Natalie's heart leaped, then settled into a staccato rhythm. Maybe once they were inside, sheltered from the wind and cold, she could unfreeze the lock on her brain and discover what it was about him that fascinated her. At least she'd have another chance to study his face. The look might have to last her a lifetime.

But first she was curious. "How did you get out of the house without me seeing you?"

"The back door." Then he added, "I was expecting you."

She was mystified, then suddenly understood. "The villagers."

"Of course." He dropped his hands from her arms and bent to pick up the field glasses. Turning back to study her for a long moment, he continued. "Perhaps you could tell me why you were spying on me."

"I told you," Natalie answered softly, her lips curving into a smile. "The *game.*"

"I still don't—" He stopped abruptly. "The puzzle." Some days he was slow, but at that moment the best he could feel was dim-witted.

And very, very angry.

Natalie nodded, her smile fading as she saw the flash of irritation swiftly followed by an angry scowl. Stanhope had warned her, but it still puzzled her that the author would resent a test of the treasure hunt.

She forced herself to relax, reasoning that there wasn't anything personal about his anger. Besides, he might be irritable by nature.

Alex lowered his eyes, shielding his expression from the woman's curious stare. Bloody hell!

The fox had arrived.

"WHY DID STANHOPE send you here?"

"He didn't." Natalie hesitated before she continued. It might be best to leave out some of the details of her mission.

"I requested your name and address," she said, taking a fortifying sip of the brandy. They had entered the house with no more words between them, and she was sensibly wary of her hostile host. Standing as close to the warming flames of the fire as she dared, she scanned her surroundings.

He had brought her into the library, a large room, with floor-to-ceiling books, a massive desk and a variety of leather chairs and sofas, all standing on intricately patterned, oriental rugs. From the untidy assortment of papers and books scattered about the room and spilling from the desk, Natalie guessed this room also served as his study. He was obviously working on another book, and she itched to sneak a look at the typed sheets that were haphazardly stacked beside the computer terminal. But a glance at her frowning host squelched the temptation.

Garrick stood a few feet away, leaning against the desk. Wide shoulders strained against the bulky knit sweater he wore, and she was distracted by thoughts of what he would look like in a dress shirt, in cashmere ... in nothing at all. Absolutely stunning, she concluded, aware that the tingling that swept her from head to toe had nothing to do with the thawing process.

Alex contemplated her every bit as intently, matching the shape of her petite form against some blueprint that seemed to have sprung, fully formed, from his mind—every curve, each delicate swell as familiar to him as his own body. He longed to reach out, to reacquaint himself with the memory—a recollection of something that had never existed.

She was, however, no illusion. That rich, auburn hair gleamed in the firelight. Eyes that had seemed so vividly brilliant in the dimness of the spring evening were clouded now, hiding her thoughts even as she openly stared. He knew he had never seen her before, had never stroked the fullness of her breast, the velvety curve at the base of her spine.

The fierce tightening he felt in his thighs was also familiar. Shifting against the desk, Alex fought against the urge to taste the lips he had never touched—knowing they would be sweet, knowing one kiss would never be enough.

Slowly, he told himself. *Very slowly.* This woman would respond to a gentle courting, a light touch. And she'd be fire underneath. Burning for him, boldly demanding everything he could give, abandoning herself to his every caress. In return she would satisfy his every wish, his every desire.

Alex had known from the first moment that he wanted her. Now he resolved to have her. Her involvement with the puzzle wouldn't get in the way. He decided to work around that and keep an eye on her progress from the best vantage point.

"What shall I call you?"

"Natalie." Her gaze focused on his radically changed expression; she realized the anger had passed. "Natalie Tracy," she added, crossing from her place by the fire to offer her hand. "As in Dick."

"Dick?" So she was involved with a man. A man named Dick. His heart thudded, and he stifled the urge to ask if she was married.

"You know." She grinned. "Dick Tracy. From the Sunday funnies."

"I beg your pardon?" Rarely had Alex felt more at a loss for words. Natalie talked in riddles.

"Never mind." Natalie shook her head, figuring this proper Englishman had never read Sunday comics. "What do I call you?"

"Garrick. Alexander Garrick." He stared at the hand she offered, bewildered for a moment by her closeness, then grasped her fingers firmly. He let her go, quickly, before he could use her hand as a lever to draw her into the circle of his arms. *Slowly,* he reminded himself. *Very slowly.*

There was still a certain Dick Tracy to deal with.

"I know." Natalie retreated to the fire, startled by the tingling that made her hand tremble—the same tingling she'd felt just moments earlier. But he'd dropped her hand, as if touching her was a distasteful chore. Putting that thought behind her, Natalie pursued the introductions. "I saw your picture on your book. But do I call you Alexander Garrick, or Mr. Garrick, or Lord Garrick or what?"

"Alex will suffice." He suppressed a smile at her irreverence toward British titles.

"Alex," she repeated, liking the feel of his name on her lips.

"So, Natalie," he said abruptly, needing a diversion from watching her moist lips mouth his name, "will Mr. Tracy be joining you soon, or is he busy wresting information from some innocent shopkeeper about me?"

"Mr. Tracy?" Now Natalie was confused. What did her father have to do with all of this?

"You know," he said, mimicking her earlier words, "Dick Tracy. From the Sunday funnies...whatever they may be."

"Comic strips," she supplied automatically, gingerly picking up the threads of conversation before she lost them altogether.

"Comic strips?" he asked, and then everything clicked as he remembered the fedora-capped detective. A comic strip, not a husband. He sighed, wishing he hadn't been so slow because the thought of a husband hadn't been a pleasant one. But then, everything seemed to be happening in slow motion since he'd met Natalie.

"Comic strips, as in cartoons. You were named after a cartoon character." He made it sound like a bizarre custom of which he didn't quite approve.

To laugh or not to laugh, that was the question. Natalie could recognize a cultural gap when it jumped up and bit her, and this was no exception. But Alex hadn't ridiculed her reference to Lord Garrick, so Natalie swallowed her giggles and let him figure out the connection by himself. But she made a mental note to dig up a few of the strips when she returned to Boston and send them to him. He might get a kick out of them.

"So if there is no Dick Tracy, I take it you are not married."

"I'm married to my job." Natalie didn't think to tell him to mind his own business. She was too busy wondering how he'd made that rather formidable jump in logic from no Dick Tracy to no marriage. Besides, talking with Alex was the most fun she'd had in months.

"Tell me why you wanted to find me." Setting the empty snifter to one side, he folded his arms across his chest and braced his thighs against the desk, crossing his feet at the ankles. If their earlier exchanges were any indication, this would take a while; he settled down to await her explanation.

"Because meeting you could be a great help." Natalie was surprised he hadn't figured that out for himself. Perhaps he couldn't see that whatever puzzle he'd devised would be a reflection of himself. Knowing the author would give her an insight into his thinking.

"You believed that meeting me would help you?" he repeated, his neutral tone giving away none of his inner thoughts.

"Naturally," she said, pleased to see he wasn't objecting. "Of course, anyone else could do the same by using a little ingenuity and common sense. I just took a shortcut and asked Stanhope."

"I see. The time limit." He had to admit her logic was faultless.

Natalie nodded her head, encouraged.

Alex understood, at least he thought he did. He *had* put a lot of himself into the puzzle, especially the clues about Oxford. He'd done his postgraduate work there and had freely drawn upon recollection and personal experience. He made a mental note to call Dempsey Press and remind the blabbermouths of their agreement to keep his identity a secret. The last thing he needed was for Foxfoot to be deluged with treasure seekers, looking for Gregory Lewis alias Alexander Garrick.

"Did you think that I would help you cheat?"

3

INCANDESCENT POOLS of emerald flame smoldered beneath lashes that couldn't hide the blaze of her outrage. Her fingers became fists, tight balls of anger that underscored this affront to her honor. She didn't speak, retaining the last bit of control that kept her from surging over the edge. But even in silence she was the epitome of furious indignation. And without a doubt, all of her wrath was focused on Alex.

She was magnificent, just as he'd known she would be. Yes, she had fire. And a temper to match. Alex knew he'd never deliberately fan those particular flames again. At least not without cause. There were better outlets for the passion inside her.

"I'm sorry," he said simply, not really sure how to defuse the situation he had created. He didn't make the mistake of moving toward her, however. He wasn't altogether confident she was totally in control, and it didn't take a brilliant mind to realize her fists were just as capable of lashing out as any man's.

She didn't appear to hear what he said, so he repeated it. "I apologize. It was an unforgivable thing to say."

Natalie continued to pretend she hadn't heard him, easily controlling the impulse to relax her fists and accept his apology. Never had she been so insulted! Well, perhaps she had been, but nothing came immediately to mind. She heard him apologize, twice, but it wasn't enough. She wanted revenge.

It would be nice to see him grovel, she thought, then immediately dismissed the idea. This man, who made her tingle from head to toe, who provoked the staccato beat of her heart . . . no, she would never want to see such a man on his knees.

He would never grovel.

But he would have to say he was sorry, just once more. That was only fair, she decided.

"No, I won't say it again."

Natalie's gaze swept over his adamant features and she believed him. He had made a mistake and apologized immediately. Twice. That was as much as she would get.

It hadn't really been an insult, but a logical question about her motives. After all, he didn't know her, and considering her job and his involvement in the puzzle, it only made sense that he might consider she would cheat. She never would, but he wasn't expected to know that.

Admitting defeat and understanding with a tired sigh, Natalie acknowledged the point. "It's all right." She shrugged casually, attempting to smile. "I probably deserved that for spying on you, anyway."

"Which raises the question of why you didn't just come to the door?"

Natalie explained her lack of success in the village that morning. "The way my luck was going, I figured I wouldn't get past your housekeeper."

"You have a point," he admitted. "You couldn't get in, so you waited for me to come out."

"Something like that," she said, then grinned. "It worked."

"Yes," he agreed, suddenly slowing his voice to a husky drawl. "It worked."

Natalie flushed at the suggestive tone, wishing her imagination would confine itself to work and leave her personal life alone. He was looking at her as if he was only barely restraining himself from leaning toward her, from touching her, from kissing her. Nonsense! She must be fantasizing. He hadn't even wanted to shake her hand.

Natalie cleared her throat, thrusting aside the strange sensation of not being in control. "I get the impression you're not too thrilled to see me."

"It's not you," he said. *Never you.* "It's what you're here to do."

"What bothers you about the test?" she asked, genuinely curious about his objections to what seemed to her the publisher's perfectly logical requirement. His answer wouldn't make any difference to her approach, of course. She couldn't afford to take his personal objections into consideration. But she wanted to know.

"Actually I have three objections. It's too late. It's not in the contract. And it's impossible," he said. "It's late, because it might hold up publication until next year. That causes some problems." Nothing he couldn't handle, but an inconvenience, all the same.

"But my deadline allows for publication this year," she returned, reaching for the brandy snifter she had set on the mantel earlier. It was empty, and Alex moved immediately to refill it.

Speaking to her over his shoulder, he said flatly, "Not when you can't solve the puzzle."

When you can't solve the puzzle. She repeated the phrase to herself. Natalie was more amused than offended by his blatant disregard for her talents as an investigator. But then, perhaps he wasn't aware of her reputation.

"Don't you think Dempsey Press has the right to impose a test?" she asked, pursuing his objections with tolerant optimism. Knowing precisely how he ranked her chances would make her victory infinitely more satisfying *when*, not *if*, she found the treasure.

He shook his head vehemently, splashing some brandy into his own glass and taking a swallow. "No, I do not. Before they purchased the publication rights, we sat down and went over the puzzle, piece by piece. They understood everything then, agreed it would work, that it met all the requirements of difficulty but recognized that someone would eventually solve it. If they had wanted a test, they should have done it earlier."

"Is that why you're angry?"

"Angry is a little harsh. Let us just say I'm frustrated!"

"There's that," Natalie conceded with just enough of a grin to make him look at her questioningly. But the hint of mischief disappeared in a flash.

His hot, hungry gaze took her by surprise. This was no trick of her imagination, no fantasy, she realized with a sudden burst of excitement. This was real.

She'd thought he was indifferent, believed he found touching her distasteful. But now, melting before the unmistakable desire that flared in his eyes, all Natalie could remember was the gentle touch of his fingers in her hair, the sensuous brush of his hand against her face.

She needed time to cope with this unexpected explosion of feelings. But time was something she couldn't afford to waste. Not now, not on the eve of the biggest challenge of her career. Natalie felt torn apart by something she didn't recognize, a force that pulled at her emotions and pushed aside her common sense. The job, she reminded herself. The job.

She redirected his attention to the puzzle. "So when I solve it in three weeks, there won't be a problem."

"The puzzle was not designed to be solved in three weeks!" he exclaimed. Particularly not during these three weeks, he added silently, turning away to shift another log onto the fire. She didn't have the slightest chance of finishing her task, not with the end of the Oracle missing.

The irritation that had plagued Alex for the past few days suddenly disappeared, replaced by anticipation. He was excited by the thought of having Natalie close, of learning what it was about her that made him want her as he'd never wanted another woman. He knew nothing about her, but that didn't matter.

They had three weeks. Alex hoped it was enough.

Giving the log a final poke, he assumed a neutral expression and turned away from the fire just in time to see the sudden light of comprehension dawn in her eyes.

It wasn't designed to be solved in three weeks. So that was it! His pride was hurt because Dempsey Press had put a time limit on Natalie's job, a time limit they deemed possible and that Alex felt was insulting. With wicked pleasure she decided that now was not the time to tell him about the head start she already had on the clue locations.

"Maybe I'm better than you think," she said to goad him.

"I doubt it." Tossing off the last of the brandy, he turned to face her. "It is not a question of how good you are, how fast you can move, or how hard you try." Taking the few steps that separated them, he was close enough to touch her. "It just can't be done. Not yet."

And because she didn't—couldn't—understand, he sighed heavily. She would take the defeat as a personal failure. But if she played his game, it was the only possible outcome.

"When do you begin?" he asked.

"Begin?"

"The puzzle. Or have you already started?"

"No. Not yet," she answered. "The three weeks begin day after tomorrow. In the meantime I'm supposed to be learning to drive and getting some rest." *I'd rather spend the time with you*, she thought, wishing for the impossible, knowing it could never be. Brushing her tongue over the suddenly dry curve of her lower lip, she wondered what it would be like to kiss him.

"We could spend tomorrow together," he said, as if it made no difference whether she accepted or not.

"Here at your house?" Natalie asked the first thing that came into her mind, her thoughts skidding madly out of control. *How did you know?* Natalie almost panicked, startled once again by his ability to guess what she most wanted.

"If you like. I can show you around," he replied, chuckling at her loss of direction. "But I was planning to start with Foxfoot, though, and then perhaps give you a tour of the area. Most tourists find it worth the effort."

"Why?" she finally asked, hoping it was a logical question. By the satisfied gleam in his eyes, she knew Alex was getting more than entertainment value for his efforts.

"Why do tourists...?" he led, fully anticipating what she would say next. It seemed they couldn't have a conversation without a minimum of red herrings and false trails, and Alex couldn't have been happier. It had been too long since a woman had been interesting enough for him to make the effort at more than conventional conversation.

"No, Alex," she corrected patiently. "Why do you want to spend tomorrow with me?" Natalie wasn't foolish enough to imagine that he wanted to spend a whole day with her for the same reasons she wanted to spend the time with him. What did he want from her that he couldn't get elsewhere? And, just as important, what did it have to do with the puzzle?

"Because the day after, you have to go to work."

Natalie's eyes closed in frustration. He wasn't going to tell her. Either that, or he was going to make her work so hard for the answer that she'd be too exhausted to realize she'd found it. Taking a deep breath, then letting it out slowly, Natalie struggled to keep her excitement at bay. *A whole day with Alex. Did she dare?*

"I'm staying in the village," she said, giving in to what she wanted.

"I know," he said and smiled, gently reminding Natalie that there was very little he didn't know.

Natalie tried to persuade herself that he didn't—couldn't—know everything. He couldn't know how much she wanted him. He couldn't.

"THIS IS EXACTLY what England is supposed to look like."

"I suppose that's another reason so many tourists like the Cotswolds," Alex agreed, pulling the Land-Rover to a stop at the crest of the hill. "Quaint villages with their weathered stone cottages and picturesque high streets, endless fields lined by stone walls, hedgerows bordering every path and road," he said, reeling off the more obvious charms of his home ground. "Perfect fodder for tourists and the like."

She grinned, acknowledging the truth of his words without challenging them. This was a terrific spot for tourists, and Natalie couldn't imagine how anyone could count their tour of England complete without a night or two at an ancient inn or classic, Cotswold manor.

Selfishly she was delighted that Alex lived off the beaten track, away from the hordes of camera-crazy sightseers. Foxfoot had somehow managed to avoid the perennial invasion and retained a unique peacefulness.

Alex shifted gears and guided the Land-Rover down the hill. "We missed morning coffee, but there should be something open for lunch if you're hungry." He was tired of dividing his attention between Natalie and the road. The hours were slipping away, and he found himself falling deeper under her spell.

Natalie grabbed the edge of her seat as the vehicle gathered speed, nodding in agreement without taking her eyes off the spectacular scenery before them. She didn't dare look directly at the road. Alex drove the Land-Rover like a race car—a bit out of control and much too fast for comfort.

"I was supposed to practice driving today," she finally protested as the truck careened around another hairpin turn. It wasn't that she didn't trust Alex, she told herself. It was the Land-Rover that she was unsure of. And after being subjected to several hours of his slightly mad approach to driving, she was beginning to suspect she might have fared better in her little rental car.

"I thought you'd like this better," he said, diving into the first parking place he saw. "With the hedgerows so tall, you can't see over them in your car. The Land-Rover gives you a few more inches."

Alex jumped from the driver's seat and rounded the bonnet to help her down. It wasn't a height of serious concern, but that didn't matter. It gave him an opportunity to touch her, if only for a moment, and he wasn't about to let a single chance escape him.

Besides, Natalie seemed to enjoy the attention.

Grasping her by the waist, he steadied her as she slid off the high seat and dropped lightly to the ground. Alex resisted the temptation to pull her close. Just a few inches closer and he would feel the softness of her breasts against his chest, the strength of her thighs.

Natalie let her hands drift from his shoulders where they had rested for precious moments, lightly passing her fingers over the soft hide of his sheepskin jacket. Another opportunity lost, she mused. He was polite, helpful and courteous. In a word, distant. He touched her as he would a maiden aunt, never holding her a moment longer than necessary, his casual courtesy defying Natalie to want more.

Biting back a sigh of disappointment, she hid her thoughts and stepped aside as he slammed the door. *What did she expect?* she asked herself. Following Alex into a nearby pub, Natalie wished she could answer the question.

Was she waiting for him to confess that his reasons for wanting to be with her had something to do with the puzzle? Or did she expect him to make wild, passionate love to her?

"Which would you prefer?"

Silently, unable to help herself, she answered, the latter, then climbed out of the fog of introspection. "Which what?"

He smiled, just as if he knew what she'd been thinking. "Which pie, Natalie? Chicken and mushroom, or the steak and kidney?"

"Chicken and mushroom, please," she answered promptly. "I know I'm supposed to do the traditional thing and try the steak and kidney pie because, after all, I am in England, and to be a proper tourist one must try all the native food, but I'm not a tourist and I really can't abide kidneys and . . ." She let it hang there, well aware she had been babbling.

Alex merely nodded, as if he agreed with her assessment of tradition in general and kidneys in particular. He gave their order at the bar, then returned with two, brimming pints of lager.

Natalie took a sip and licked the foam from her upper lip. She liked it. More importantly, it gave her something to do besides stare at Alex.

Alex watched the pink tip of her tongue dart out and clean the foam from her lip, fascinated by the unconscious movement. He was tempted to offer his assistance. Instead he asked her about her job.

She stiffened at the unexpected question. A hard, cold knot formed at the bottom of her stomach, letting her know—just in case she was tempted to ignore her better judgment—that this was what he had wanted all along.

Alex had had nearly a full day's practice in reading her expressions. Otherwise he might have missed the sudden hurt that flashed deep in her eyes before it was buried. She was learning to hide her emotions before they could be used against her. Not that he would ever use what he could see that way. But Natalie didn't know that.

He tried to make his tone genuinely inquisitive. It was, perhaps, the only thing he could do to persuade her his questions were harmless. Even though he had discovered most of the answers for himself the previous evening, during a lengthy telephone conversation with a well-placed contact, he still wanted to hear Natalie's version.

Besides, this was more for her benefit than for his. Getting her to relax and to stay relaxed was proving more difficult than he had anticipated. She was suspicious, as she probably had a right to be, and hadn't yet decided to accept his interest as personal. Until she did, there was nothing he could do that would convince her.

But talking would be a step in the right direction. She might even throw in something he didn't know and make the exercise productive. "What do you want to know?"

"Your job," he finally repeated. "For a start, it would be interesting to know what it is. And if you don't mind answering that, we might discuss things like which university you attended, where you live, and what you like to do in your free time."

"I won't argue about the puzzle," she insisted.

"Did I *ask* you about the treasure hunt?" He spread his hands in a timeless gesture of benign innocence.

Natalie was saved from replying by the arrival of their meals. Eyeing him over the steaming pie, she debated whether or not to believe him, and suddenly decided it didn't matter. She was certainly going to avoid the subject of the treasure hunt, so he could try until he was blue in the face to get information about it—if that was his goal. On the other hand, this might be an opportunity to learn a few things about Alex.

"Will you talk about yourself?" Natalie asked.

"I'll answer questions," he said obliquely.

She thought about it, then nodded. "I do private investigations. Mostly we're concerned with things that people have lost or misplaced. Occasionally we handle cases of missing people."

From what he had learned from a few well-placed phone calls, Natalie owned the agency and had expanded it from a simple lost and found enterprise to a much respected business. Alex carefully stifled his grin and pushed for something a little more detailed. "You mean things like divorce cases, where the husband disappears and the wife is trying to sue for desertion?"

Natalie grimaced at his misunderstanding, then admitted it was her own fault. "No, we don't get involved in divorce cases. The people end of the business is normally concerned with finding missing children." She explained how that part of the business had expanded, regrettably so, in the last few years. "We've got a good reputation for getting results, whether it's locating children who've been taken out of the state by one parent, or who've run away from home."

"I can't decide if you like doing that or not," he said carefully. "You're telling me facts, without any feeling." Surprised when he looked down and saw his plate was empty, he moved it aside and persisted. "If I didn't know you any better, I'd say you found that type of work disagreeable."

Natalie's chin jerked up, and she found him watching her. She was startled by his perception, almost frightened that he could see so easily what others had missed. It was true. She did try to keep herself distant from that end of the business. While the results were often rewarding, she found herself more productive in other areas. She loved following paper trails, searching for legitimate heirs, long lost brothers or even old, but not forgotten loves.

The search for lost children ripped her heart to shreds.

"You're right. I hate that part of it. I give those cases to the other investigators, who are good at it." Natalie twisted the fork between her fingers. "It's not that I can't do it. I've done it, several times. But at the end of each case I'm so drained by the process that I can't work for days. And I'm no good to the agency that way."

"Why does it bother you so much?" he asked quietly.

"Because I can't help but imagine that it's my own child out there, alone, defenseless, hurt. I empathize with the parents, live through their anguish with them, share in their misery." Lifting her gaze once again to meet his, she confessed, "It's sheer agony to pretend a professional distance that simply isn't there."

"What are you afraid of, Natalie?"

Before she could stop herself, she answered him. "I'm afraid that if I continue to work on those cases, I'll never have a child of my own."

4

"EXPLAIN."

It was a demand, not a request. But Natalie complied; she had opened the subject, and it was up to her to close it.

"Not because I don't want one. But because I'll be too frightened to bring one into the world." Natalie took a deep breath, then another, before returning her gaze to meet his. "That's why I don't do those cases anymore."

Laughter from a nearby table snapped her out of the somber mood and brought a bright flush of embarrassment to her cheeks. She'd never confessed that before. Alex must think she was a real fruitcake.

Chancing a glance in his direction, she saw something quite different. Another loud guffaw came from the bar, and she changed the topic. "I generally concentrate on finding things, not people. I'm good at it."

"I see," he said, as if suddenly understanding why Natalie had been chosen to find the treasure.

"Yes." And that, she hoped, was as close as they would come to the subject of the puzzle.

"Your employer must be quite understanding to permit you to work only in the areas you desire," he prodded.

"There's that," she agreed, smiling at her secret. She didn't want to tell him she was the owner of the very successful agency. It would be bragging.

Alex masked his surprise. Personal success wasn't normally something people were shy about discussing, and he'd been told Natalie had more to be proud of than most. But he let it slide, and continued asking questions about the part of the job that she liked.

"So now I understand why you're in England," he said, satisfied that he had learned as much about her professional life as he could without seeming excessively curious. "Your parents?"

"They're safely tucked away in California," she said, "savoring retirement, combined with managing a craft shop just north of Carmel. They're in heaven, and I'm marking the time before they start demanding I join them." Then she tried to turn the tables. "And yours?"

"In France," he countered.

"And?"

"And what?" But he smiled, giving in to her obvious hint that it was his turn to talk. "They moved there years ago, while they were still young enough to enjoy the food and old enough to afford it. They let me buy the house so I could call it mine, then put the money into a trust fund for their first grandchild," he supplied, grimacing at the memory. He'd been tricked on that particular transaction, and was still looking for a way to get his own back. Irrespective of their generosity, Alex didn't like their heavy-handed hints that they wanted him to start a family.

"Do you like writing thrillers?"

"Yes," he replied succinctly, then countered, "Did you leave someone behind who . . . misses you?"

"Yes," she responded without hesitation. "My secretary." Natalie didn't mention any of the men she'd dated over the last few months, if that was what he really wanted to know, because at the moment she couldn't even remember their names.

"A she?"

"Yes," Natalie affirmed, then took pity on his air of confusion. "We're great friends. And she runs the office, so I hope she misses me. Are you writing another?"

"Yes."

"Thriller?" *For God's sake, don't let it be another puzzle book.* Natalie couldn't cope with that.

"Of course."

A boisterous crowd burst through the pub door, and Alex stood up, suddenly anxious to leave the restaurant. Guiding Natalie back into the sunshine, he dodged the sheepdog tied up at the pub entrance and headed back to the Land-Rover.

"What do you want to see this afternoon?" he asked, once again assuming the role of tour guide.

"You're the expert." But her attention was on an enormous bowl and pitcher displayed in a shop window across the street. Needing a closer look, she pulled her elbow out of Alex's grasp and dashed into the traffic, ignoring the blaring horn as she leaped to safety on the other side.

Alex was forced to follow.

"You shouldn't do things like that in this country!" he snapped.

"Things like what?" Natalie asked absently, her attention on the pitcher.

"Like ducking into the traffic," he said heatedly. "You scared ten years off me!"

Natalie finally saw the price tag dangling from the pitcher's handle, multiplied the pounds sterling by the current rate of exchange, and decided she could live without it. Turning to Alex, she pretended to examine his face, then grinned. "You don't seem to be the worse for wear, Alex."

"I'll show you worse for wear!" he threatened.

Not the least bit intimidated, Natalie nevertheless thought it best to change the subject. "Would you let me drive, so I can get some practice in?"

"You must be mad!"

Natalie shrugged. Englishmen were so conservative sometimes. "Then I'll just have to settle for the occasional vista over the hedgerow, won't I?"

"That's correct," Alex agreed before pulling her away from the window. "If you're lucky, that is. I might just make you ride behind, with the spare tire and the rest of the gear, if I don't calm down before then."

"And dead bodies?" she queried, knowing that was where thriller writers often transported their victims.

"Dead bodies?" Alex pulled up short, torn between studying the traffic for an opportunity to cross and wondering what she was talking about. But Natalie didn't deign to answer, so he concentrated on the traffic, and in no time they were back in the Land-Rover.

"Onward, James," she commanded.

James? Where had he come from? Alex wondered as he reached forward to turn on the ignition. "Oh, hell!" Alex slumped over the steering wheel, knocking his forehead repeatedly against the hard plastic.

"Lost your key?" she inquired.

"Just my license," he replied, straightening from the wheel before cranking the window open. With a long string of curses that Natalie understood only in context, he pulled the cellophane-wrapped notice from beneath the windshield wipers and tossed it onto the floor.

"Bad news?"

"I'm a repeat offender. That means they usually go looking for me when their quotas are low," he growled, throwing the Land-Rover into gear and fighting his way into the traffic.

"I didn't know they used quotas in England."

"Quotas are universal, Natalie."

"What makes you think you've lost your license?" she asked, knowing that in the U.S., at least, a person didn't get grounded—or whatever—for collecting a disproportionate number of parking tickets.

"Because the magistrate advised me the next time I got a ticket, I would be up before him at the Old Bailey." He wasn't sure the threat had been an exaggeration.

"Old Bailey?"

"As in Supreme Court."

"Oh." Natalie was suitably impressed. "Would it help if I said I was driving and copped the ticket?"

"Copped the ticket?"

"Yeah. As in took the blame, threw myself on the mercy of the court and pleaded for leniency?" Natalie liked the idea of that, especially since a parking violation in England seemed insignificant against her collection of jaywalking tickets.

"You'd do that?"

"Why not?" she asked, regretting only that she didn't know what the punishment was in England for a parking ticket.

He grinned. "I like it."

"Thought you might," she affirmed, then clutched the well-worn leather that was her seat cushion. Alex had regained his confidence at the wheel, and Natalie was smart enough to concentrate on survival.

AS HE WATCHED the Land-Rover pull into traffic and head back up the high street, Ned Murdoch smiled.

This was going to be easier than he had thought. Much easier.

If scaring Natalie Tracy was the object of the exercise, then the opportunities should be plentiful. If Stanhope decided more than a scare was necessary, that, too would be simple.

The woman didn't suspect she was being followed, nor did she take even rudimentary care when doing something as routine as crossing the street.

He wondered what Stanhope would do when he told him that the woman had spent the day with Garrick. Perhaps it would be necessary to do more than scare her, especially if it became apparent that Garrick was interfering.

If they had to get rid of the woman, that left the question of what to do about Garrick. He could be very busy over the next few days.... A smile crossed his face as he considered all the possibilities. Pleasantly busy.

"SO HOW DO WE GO ABOUT fixing your ticket?" Natalie asked between sips of brandy. Her determination to endure an entire afternoon of Alex's unique driving without complaint had almost drawn blood from the proverbial stone, and now that they were back at his home, she was in serious need of sustenance—in alcoholic form.

"You were serious?" he queried. "Nat, I appreciate the gallant gesture, but . . ."

"But you lose your driving license if I don't. You admitted as much."

"Very well. Just give me your license number, and I'll leave it with the local constable. With luck, they'll believe you borrowed the Land-Rover and committed the offense behind my back."

"That'll work." she agreed. "If not, let me know and I'll check in with the local magistrate in Oxford."

"Oxford?" The spark of interest in his slightly raised eyebrows almost panicked her. After an entire day of avoiding the puzzle, she had inadvertently mentioned it.

Natalie was so irritated with herself that she almost bit her tongue off. She'd just told Alex where she was beginning her attempt to solve the puzzle, definitely the wrong move.

"I understand they have good bookstores," she lied brightly. "I thought I'd drop by there, first thing tomorrow, on my way to..." She purposely let her words dangle, pretending that her next stop was a huge secret. "Besides, I thought we weren't discussing the game."

"You're right," he agreed, then proceeded to identify the best booksellers. "Blackwell's on Broad Street keeps a wide selection, just about anything you'd want, and there's a new shop at the other end of the street that might be helpful." He fell silent, trying to avoid bringing up the subject of the treasure hunt again. Alex studied the woman before him. She enchanted him and bewildered him.

He wanted her.

He couldn't, of course. Not yet. Today had been only a beginning, though a good one.

But just a taste, he promised himself. He couldn't let her leave, not without a taste. Silently he closed the distance between them.

Natalie watched him take her brandy and setting his own aside, hardly aware of the almost rhythmic pop and crackle of the fire a few feet away. Every nerve, every sense was focused on the man bending toward her.

She wanted him to touch her, needed to touch him, to feel his lips against hers. Was he real or a fantasy she had created on that windswept hill? She didn't know and suddenly, it didn't matter. His mouth covered hers, and Natalie was swept into the heat of desire. He moved his lips over hers, his teeth nipping at the fullness of her mouth, his tongue reaching out to soothe the tantalizing hurts. His kisses were demanding, greedy.

Natalie was fueled by her own need, totally responsive to his demands, hungry for his strength. She closed her eyes against the urgency she read in his, unable to fight what she'd never felt before. Strong hands swept impatiently across her shoulders, down her arms, then back up again to hold her steady for his kisses. In a movement that was as natural as it was necessary, Natalie raised her arms to his shoulders, locking her hands behind his neck in a desperate effort to get closer to the fire that was burning inside him, that was consuming her.

Alex didn't stop to persuade Natalie to open her mouth to him. With a firm pressure on her jaw, he forced his way past the barrier of her teeth, then pushed his tongue into her sweet warmth. He was too much in a hurry, too excited about what lay inside to take things slowly.

He had expected fire from her. He got lightning.

Slowly. Alex pushed aside the thought, devouring the recesses of her mouth, coaxing her tongue into an erotic game of stroke and thrust. One hand tangled in the mass of hair at her nape, holding her mouth roughly to his. The other hand briefly caressed the flat planes of her back before dipping to the swell of her bottom. He couldn't stop himself from drawing her closer, cupping his large hand against her womanly shape and pulling her to meet the hardness between his thighs.

His chest tightened against the building pressure, and he groaned agonizingly into her mouth, his tongue thrusting in a rhythm that matched the pulse in the hard need that nestled against her belly. The heat was building, searing him, burning . . . !

"Damn!" He pulled Natalie away from the log that had rolled off the burning fire. With movements that were very nearly painful, he left her alone, grabbed the tongs that were hanging above the hearth and managed to return the flaming piece of wood to where it belonged. With the aid of the poker he readjusted the pile, taking his time now. He'd been so absorbed in his own needs that he hadn't taken proper care in setting the log on the fire.

Slowly. Yes, there was that, too.

Straightening away from the fireplace, he turned to see her watching him, her lips moist and swollen from his assault, her hair in tangles across one shoulder. The passion in her was on the surface, waiting for him.

He knew instinctively that she would come to his bed. That knowledge made the waiting harder. But he also knew she would regret it tomorrow, that she was still unsure.

He was going to change that.

Slowly. That was important. He wanted their first time together to be perfect, to be an erotic voyage she'd never forget. By pleasing Natalie, he could keep her with him until his body no longer ached with the needs she'd created in him.

Working around the demands of the puzzle would be tricky, but he was confident he could. Alex admitted now that he couldn't talk her out of chasing after the treasure, and contrarily it pleased him that her sense of honor would keep her on the trail. Her days would be filled with the intricacies of the game.

That didn't mean he couldn't share her nights.

Alex wanted her fire, her passion. Because he wanted it all, he would move slowly.

"The rug," she said, pointing to the scorched spot.

"Never mind it."

Natalie was breathless, unable to find words to describe what was happening inside her. Perhaps that was just as well, she thought, wondering why he was looking at her that way, reserve clouding his eyes, the magically warm lips drawing into a firm line of stubborn determination. The taste of his mouth was still on her lips, the warmth of his caresses not forgotten.

But *he* had forgotten. Standing apart from her now, hands thrust deep into his pockets, Alex was obviously not interested in continuing what they had started. Natalie felt herself flushing. She should have known better, of course, but her previous experiences with men had never provoked such an abandoned response. Obviously, the fireworks had been one-sided.

Then why had it felt so right?

"It's probably best if you leave now," he said quietly. "It will be better this way."

She nodded, her eyes not quite meeting his. Then Natalie turned and walked toward the door, shoulders squared against the hurt that gnawed at her insides. The pain she felt must be pride, she thought distractedly. Pride or ego. Either way he had rejected her.

It hurt like hell.

"My housekeeper will drive you," Alex said from behind her, startling Natalie into looking at him. Again she saw the hunger, the need. Or thought she saw them. But she must have been mistaken, because when she blinked the want was gone. Wishful thinking, she admitted, cursing her vivid imagination. But there was strength inside her now, a spirit that wouldn't let him see the humiliation she was suffering. Pride—she let him have a good look at that. It made her strong, gave her the willpower to walk away.

"Will you have lunch with me tomorrow?" he asked quietly, holding himself quite still.

"Why?" What was he trying to do? He had kissed her, then rejected her. And now he wanted to see her again. There could only be one purpose behind his invitation. It had to be the puzzle. Was he trying to divert her from pursuing the hunt?

Did he think he could distract her so easily? Had he learned nothing about her that day?

"Because I want to see you again," he said, grateful to see the wounded look leave her face, though it was replaced by anger.

Natalie took a deep breath, then met his eyes. The anger steadied her, bringing with it a dash of reason. Yes, anger was a useful tool, but even that wouldn't last. Being in the same room—the same town—with him was dangerous. She had to leave, put some distance between temptation and herself.

"Lunch?" she repeated in a voice coated with sugar, calling on a veneer of sophistication that she'd never known herself to be capable of. "I'd love to, Alex." Her eyes skipped over his startled expression as she reached for her coat and gloves.

Alex knew she was up to something; her easy acceptance masked what she was really planning. It didn't matter. She couldn't run far. He would find her. In the meantime he named a restaurant in Oxford and gave her directions—not that he expected her to be there.

The chase would make things just that much more exciting, for both of them.

5

NATALIE DIVED HEADFIRST into the brambles at the side of the road, swallowing the Land-Rover's dust as it sped by without stopping. She could just hear the vanishing roar of the engine as she began to check for breaks and bruises, and used up her entire vocabulary of cuss words—twice—before she finally stood up. Obviously Alex wasn't the only lousy driver in England, but somehow she wasn't comforted by the thought.

Resolving to limit the remainder of her morning jog to the pedestrian byways of the village, Natalie spared a final, black thought for the reckless driver and resumed a steady pace—only slightly influenced by a twinge in her knee.

It was a pity about Foxfoot, she thought a while later when she stopped in the middle of the bridge. Taking deep, steadying breaths, she leaned her elbows on the rough stone, peering over the sturdy parapet into the clear water below.

Yes, it was a darned shame she'd never come back here. Mad drivers aside, it was a lovely place, especially with the sun's morning rays slanting between the gray stone houses. With its system of ancient bridges that criss-crossed the meandering stream, Foxfoot was an ideal spot for running, since most of the automobile traffic was directed around the town. Although Natalie was out early, she wasn't alone. The village had come alive as she ran through the winding streets. Shopkeepers raised their awnings against the early-morning glare, calling good-morning as she passed.

This casual acceptance made her feel good. Too bad she had to leave. With a last look into the freezing water, Natalie shoved herself away from the wall and tried not to limp the last few yards to the front door of the inn.

Returning to her room was easier than she had thought it would be, especially as she had been so eager to escape just an hour earlier. But the physical demands the run had made on her body had released the tensions that had kept her from sleeping. Natalie felt renewed, alive with the anticipation of another day.

YESTERDAY EVENING, in the inn's lounge, Natalie had opened *The Quest*, determined to salvage her pride, goaded by the need to prove she could do what Alex had said was impossible. She had spent hours studying the puzzle, trying to banish Alex from her thoughts.

She would prove him wrong. She would solve his puzzle.

The puzzle was a jumbled series of clues and locations, with two pages dedicated to each place. With no text, the clues were pictures that looked more as if they belonged in a child's book than a guide to a treasure hunt for adults. Neil Stanhope had pointed out to her the place-names that were the keys to each illustration.

The names and pictures were all she had to go on. But it was enough. It had to be.

The manuscript pages were not in any particular order, she guessed. The Oxford clue was a drawing of a university gown, its collar and style unique to that university.

Natalie had set to work, studying the other illustrations on the page, trying to determine a logical starting point. The main picture focused on a man seated at a pottery wheel, his hands holding a clay vase or cup on the spinning surface. He sat near an open door, the light from the room beaming across the threshold, the stars outside shining brightly. In the garden stood a sundial.

Inside the house, near the potter's feet, was a group of small animals—rabbits, squirrels and foxes. The only other distinguishable feature was a table. It was round, apparently not meant to be part of the furnishings, but rather an abstract drawing in the corner of the small room. In the center of the table a horse reared up on its hind legs. It was ringed by a series of wooden benches.

That was all, except for the university gown that regally draped one of the rabbits. Only a wash of color as background brightened the drawings, bringing them together into one cohesive unit.

She had listed the items: *starry sky, door, sundial, round table with horse, animals, potter, wheel, clay.* Natalie didn't think the vase or cup was important, because she couldn't really tell what it was.

Nothing had jumped out at her, but then, she hadn't expected the puzzle to be easy. *What item was out of place?* she asked herself. It was the logical place to start. The sky was okay, the doorway reasonable, the potter and wheel seemed normal.

Three things had struck her as odd.

The round table with the horse on it. Was there a round table in Oxford, perhaps a famous table in a college? The horse reminded Natalie of the story of King Arthur, when the knights had rebelled and if she remembered correctly, ridden their mounts on top of the famous Round Table, destroying the symbol of Arthur's reign. But what did that have to do with Oxford? Natalie made a note to check her books for any mention of King Arthur or another round table.

The animals—the rabbits, squirrels and foxes—were normally found out-of-doors and, therefore, were next on her list. They might indicate a zoo or an animal sanctuary. Natalie had considered the clue too vague and set it aside.

Then there was the sundial. Under the night sky it was an incongruous element. Why would Alex have drawn a sundial at night, when it couldn't be read?

Gathering her books and notes and shoving them into her carryall, Natalie had headed back to her room. It hadn't been late, still on the minus side of midnight. But she'd greedily sought the quiet of the night, the comfort of darkness.

Lying in her bed under the inn's steeply pitched roof, Natalie had at last let her defenses slip. Vibrant, painful and furious, her emotions had assaulted her, the tortured images of the afternoon slamming at her from all sides, swinging almost viciously from the moment of Alex's embrace to his rejection of her. So sweet, so painful.

She had let the hurt and pain wash over her, believing that by doing so she could get the pain out of her system, leaving the memories intact—clear, but painless.

They were all she would ever have.

AT TEN O'CLOCK that same spring morning, Natalie stood before the dark, imposing entrance to the old Bodleian Library, impatiently waiting for a gaggle of tourists to file out through the tiny doorway cut into the larger panel. An hour earlier, she had arrived at the door of the tourist information office, justifiably proud of herself for having successfully negotiated the network of one-way streets that comprised downtown Oxford. She'd decided to find the hotel later, too excited to slow her pace for the mundane things.

"Do you have a list of sundials?" Only in England could she ask such a question, she mused.

The young girl behind the desk flashed her a friendly smile. "Are you looking for sundials all over England, or just in Oxford?"

"Just Oxford, I hope." Maybe the question hadn't been so out of line, after all!

"I don't have a list of sundials just for Oxford."

"But you have one for England?" Natalie pressed.

"No," the girl replied innocently, as if she'd never suggested such a thing.

"But why did you ask if I wanted it for Oxford or for England?"

"I was curious. I've never had a request for sundials before." The girl smiled, apparently encouraging Natalie to continue the conversation.

Natalie took a deep breath, then tried again. "I'm looking for sundials, probably in Oxford. Can you give me some idea where to look?"

"Of course," the girl replied, as if it was the first time she'd heard the request. Then she proceeded to pull a variety of tourist brochures from the rack behind her, adding a handwritten list of other possible places where Natalie might find sundials—a list that began with nearly forty colleges. Her hands filled with miscellaneous brochures and a list of the times various colleges and sights were open, Natalie managed to thank the girl and escape the small office.

Just a few yards away, Natalie found a bench where she could stop and study the information. It took only moments to realize she was in the wrong place at the wrong time. Most of the better-known sights, which opened early, were several blocks away. And while she was just steps from several of the colleges, they weren't open until after lunch. With a sigh Natalie set off down Cornmarket, en route to her first stop.

The Bodleian Library was the fourth on her list, and she discovered it was one more place in Oxford that did not boast a sundial. The first three stops had also been in vain. Now, with nothing better to do before the colleges opened, Natalie crossed her fingers and consulted her map, and headed down the narrow street toward the Botanical Gardens.

There she found her very first sundial, tucked away in a secluded corner of the garden between the river and a gravel footpath. But even from a distance, Natalie could see it looked nothing like the sundial in the book.

Flopping onto a convenient bench, Natalie gazed at the instrument with resignation.

"I'm hungry for pasta. How about you?"

She should have expected this, Natalie thought with the few wits she had left. Congratulating herself for not literally jumping out of her skin, she focused on the sundial, ignoring the man who had stolen her sleep. Maybe if she pretended he wasn't there, he would go away.

"If you'd prefer Chinese," he continued, dropping onto the bench beside her, "there's a great place near the railway station. We could be there in ten minutes."

Natalie concentrated on the sundial, then checked her watch against the stone timepiece. It was twelve-thirty, the time she had agreed to meet Alex for lunch.

Natalie tilted her head his way, noting his relaxed slouch with a touch of envy. "Lunch?" she asked innocently. Two could play at this game.

And, for the first time since he'd surprised her, Natalie brought her gaze level with his, holding his attention for just a moment before he looked away. It didn't hurt. At least, not as much as she had thought it would. Rejection had made her strong. But what she had glimpsed in his eyes was something else entirely. They conveyed an impression of amused tolerance, as if Natalie and her reactions touched a soft spot deep inside him. It was impossible, she knew, but then, she hadn't had much luck understanding him the night before.

Natalie was certain of one thing. She saw no sign of cunning, nothing to indicate he wanted anything more than her company for lunch. But ulterior motives weren't always apparent, and she remained convinced that his presence had something to do with the puzzle.

"Lunch," he repeated firmly. "I'm getting hungry. Well?" he prodded. She saw him swing his roving eyes from their casual inspection of the garden to meet hers.

Startled, Natalie forgot she was furious with him. She didn't trust him, but that didn't mean she had to avoid him. Drawing the tip of her tongue along suddenly dry lips, she tried to think of a reason to say no. But when his gaze dropped to rest on her mouth, it was impossible.

"Italian?" she managed.

Pushing himself off the bench, Alex waited for her to collect the various papers and schedules she had dragged out of her bag. How had he found her? Natalie found herself thinking. Did she really want to know? Shoving the last brochure into her shoulder bag, she turned, to find herself standing toe-to-toe with Alex. It made her nervous to be so close to him, and she blurted out the last thought that had crossed her mind.

"How did—?" She was hushed by his fingers as they rose to seal her lips. The contact was electrifying, and it took all of her willpower to stand passively under his touch.

"I told you last night. I wanted to see you again. Isn't that enough for now?" He hypnotized her with his voice, drawing his fingers across the trembling fullness of her lips as he spoke.

Natalie was confused, but the strength that had come to her in the early, predawn hours did not desert her. She was no longer weak, caught in the spell he'd woven around her. She was still caught in the same spell, but strong. There was a difference.

Lunch. What could it hurt?

"THE FIRST RULE," he began, twirling his fork in the creamy pasta, "is never to discuss *The Quest*."

"Okay." Two syllables were all she could manage at the moment. She had important things on her mind, like eating. It had been a busy morning and she was famished. Natalie believed a healthy appetite never needed an excuse.

"The second rule—"

"Nope." Things were complicated enough, and Rule #1 was sufficient.

Natalie glanced up, catching the glint of curiosity in his eyes, and was pleased that she could throw him off his stride. "No more rules," she said in a tone that brooked no argument. "I've got too much to worry about, as it is."

"Such as?" he asked, dividing his attention between his plate and the woman seated opposite him. He was incredibly lucky, this much he knew already. Though Natalie had been hurt and angry the night before, she didn't let that color her outlook today. She was willing to be with him—at least, willing with a minimum of fuss. Judging by the way she was wolfing down her food, his presence didn't affect her one way or the other.

"Such as why you followed me to Oxford. Such as why you bothered—especially after you couldn't wait to be rid of me last night. You kissed me, then rejected me. And now you've gone out of your way to take me to lunch." Shaking her head as though confronted with a deeper mystery than she could fathom, she lifted her eyes to stare into his, looking for the answer, not knowing what she might find. When she could decipher nothing, she concluded, "I can only think it has something to do with the hunt."

Alex flushed, gritting his teeth at the uncomfortable sensation. This was not the conversation he had anticipated, much less the place he would have chosen for it. What the hell was she talking about? He had *rejected her*? He had sent her home to give her time, to let her escape the demands he would have made if she had stayed. He had imagined her anger was due to his clumsy handling of the situation.

He'd been wrong. Not about the clumsiness, that was indisputable. Gulping down the rest of his wine, he recalled the scene in his home the night before, trying to see what had happened from Natalie's point of view. Finally the penny dropped.

He hoped it wasn't too late.

"I thought you understood last night," he said slowly, pushing his unfinished meal to one side. "I thought it would be better if you left, before things got out of hand."

"You didn't want me," she insisted. "So why are you here, unless you want to affect my chances of finishing the puzzle?"

"Damn the puzzle! Is that what you really believe?" he exclaimed, raising his voice in indignation.

"Nothing else makes much sense. What else is there?"

"There's us. You and me and the magic that's just waiting to happen," he said, spitting the words across the table in anger. "I sent you away last night to give you time to trust your instincts, to let you make your own decision. I told you it would be better if we waited."

"No," she said, and something inside him plummeted into infinity. "No, you didn't. You said it would be better if I left." Natalie paused, then added, "I'm not a mind reader."

Raising her eyes to meet the hot look that he didn't seem able to hide, she frowned, still too wary to respond. Understanding where everything had fallen apart was easy now. Looking at things from Alex's point of view, it all made sense. But Natalie still wasn't absolutely convinced. She'd been hurt too deeply by his rejection. Yet how could she have been so terribly hurt by a man who was practically a stranger?

No, she didn't trust him. She couldn't afford to. Not yet.

"Not want you!" he exploded. Lowering his voice to a husky growl that sent shivers zinging up and down her spine, he said. "I want you so badly that I cannot sleep. I want you so badly that it hurts. If you had given me even a little encouragement, I would have proved it to you, moments ago in the garden."

Natalie almost believed him, nearly let herself be swayed by the physical longing he provoked with his admission.

She was stuck for something to say. Nothing seemed appropriate, especially after what he'd just told her. How could she tell him she wanted him, but didn't trust him? How could she ask him to wait, fully aware the next three weeks would be a study in torture . . . not knowing if he would even be there when she finished? And if he didn't wait, then she would know he had only wanted to throw her off course, to stop her from solving the puzzle.

But luck seemed to be with her. The waitress appeared out of nowhere, retrieving the half-eaten plates of noodles with a deft motion, leaving the bill with a sleight of hand that Natalie marveled at. A glance at her watch told her the bad news.

"I've gotta go now." She scooted to the edge of the bench seat, dragging her purse in her wake.

"Yes. I know." Alex had no intention of stopping her. It was important that she believe he understood her professional priorities. He could keep an eye on her more easily if she accepted that. "Where are you staying?" he asked, finding the question easier than he had anticipated.

"Why?"

"So I haven't got to follow you around all afternoon," he said, not at all put off by the prospect. Keeping Natalie in sight, without letting her know he was there, had been fun. And even if she told him the name of her hotel, Alex knew he'd have to follow her around for the rest of the day. He didn't really expect her to tell him the truth, not yet. She didn't trust him, he could tell by the way she avoided meeting his eyes. But if Natalie believed he wouldn't bother following her, then it would be easier to do just that.

He'd followed her all morning, probably all the way from the inn. She found the idea exciting, wishing she had known he was there, watching her every move, lying in wait for the best moment to approach her.

But she couldn't afford to meet him tonight or any other night. It would be too easy to believe what he said, to fall prey to the passion he could so easily ignite.

"Have dinner with me, Natalie." He grasped her wrist to keep her from leaving without answering. "Just dinner."

Natalie gasped at the fiery contact. It made lying harder, much harder, because she wanted him to touch her again. But she straightened her spine, a physical move that strengthened her resolve to leave and to leave alone.

"The Black Horse," she said, relieved that she wasn't really telling him a lie. Liz had reserved a room for her there. Natalie just would have to find somewhere else to stay.

"I'll be there at eight."

Her wrist was suddenly cold as he released it, and she found herself massaging the sudden chill away as she stepped out to join the never-ending flow of human traffic.

Throwing down some money to settle the lunch bill, Alex skirted the few tables as he headed for the door and cautiously looked out before he joined the rush of people on the pavement. He didn't hurry; there wasn't any need. Oxford was a small town, and he'd catch sight of her sooner or later. The real problem would be to avoid bumping into her accidentally.

The bright yellow anorak she wore had been a great help that morning, and when Alex turned into High Street, he spotted the yellow beacon just ahead. Sighing contentedly, he settled down to another game of follow the leader.

She might run, but she could never hide.

THE SUNDIAL at Christ Church College was mounted on a clock tower, as were three others she found that afternoon. Natalie had toured a surprising number of colleges that boasted more than one sundial and an equal number that had none.

They were all interesting to look at, especially the one at Merton College. It was far and away the most intricate one she had seen. Unfortunately, none of them resembled the sundial in the book.

Natalie found herself caught up in a small tour group in the Fellows' Quad at Merton. The guide had been pointing out various points of interest as they passed through the maze of quads—quadrangles, they were told, courtyards to Natalie—and she had been impressed to discover that Merton was the oldest college at Oxford, founded in the thirteenth century. Marveling at the historical significance of such a place, Natalie had nearly missed the guide's reference to the "nomen" in the garden.

What was a nomen she wondered, checking surreptitiously for gnomes and other garden fairies, afraid to ask, lest she be spotted as an intruder. She needn't have worried. An American lady sporting tennis shoes and an unmistakable Brooklyn accent asked the question for her.

Nomen, spelled *gnomon*, according to the guide, was the Greek word for the shadow-throwing shaft on a sundial. And there it was, a magnificent piece of brass, shaped like a globe, with intertwining bands forming an intricate pattern. Natalie drew closer, not because it was the one in the book, but because it was a beautiful work of art.

Still, nomen or gnomon, it wasn't her sundial.

When the colleges closed their massive gates to tourists, Natalie had amassed a total of sixteen sundials, having visited all but six colleges. Her feet were sore, and there would probably be a permanent warp in her shoulder from the heavy bag she'd carried all day. Telling herself things could only get worse, she stopped at a large bookstore on the corner of Broad Street and Cornmarket and picked up a couple of volumes dealing with Oxford, one a history, the other containing more up-to-date information about the city. Carrying her purchases in one hand and balancing her shoulder bag on the opposite shoulder, she returned to the street.

Trekking to the car, Natalie fought her way through rush-hour traffic to a hotel she had found listed at the tourist information center. It took longer than she expected, mainly because all traffic was routed around the town, and everyone seemed to want to get out at the same time. Driving wasn't difficult, not with the typical British sense of fair play that allowed traffic to merge with a minimum of fuss. Still, it was slow, giving Natalie a chance to review her progress—or lack of it!

Sixteen sundials. It was impossible to believe she'd found sixteen sundials without stumbling across the one she sought. Almost against the odds, she mused, dodging a bicycle that appeared out of nowhere. Sixteen misses, no hits. What lousy luck.

Spotting the hotel just a few yards down the busy street, Natalie shot her car through a break in the traffic and into the parking lot. Relieved that she'd made the trip in one piece, she dragged her shoulder bag out of the car, leaving her suitcase on the chance there was no room at the inn.

She was in luck. Natalie signed her name in the ancient registration book, then handed her keys to the porter. "Could you please have someone bring in my suitcase?" she asked, too tired to do the job herself. "It's in the trunk."

"Trunk?" The young man looked at Natalie curiously, swinging the keys idly in one hand.

"Yes, trunk," she repeated, her mind only half on the conversation. The rest of her thoughts centered around the bathtub waiting upstairs for her tired body. "Trunk, as in back end of the car, the place where the spare tire is stored, where dead bodies end up in murder stories. You know, trunk!"

"Of course," he nodded sagely. "The boot."

"The boot?" Natalie jerked her head back to the young man, skeptical of his grasp of the conversation. "What boot?"

"Back end of the car, with the tires and dead bodies." Then he grinned and spun on his heel, whistling and swinging the keys as he headed in the direction of the parking lot.

NATALIE HELD HER BREATH, then repeated the word softly. "Nomenclator."

That had to be it! Nothing else made sense or was so clever—so bold in its very conception. It had to be the answer.

Rather, she thought, calming herself slightly, it just might be the first real clue. Carefully she reviewed the logic that had led her to the startling discovery.

Scattered across the bed were scraps of paper, each bearing the name of the objects from the picture in *The Quest*. They were all there, in as many variations as Natalie could imagine. It had been the gnomon that had first given her the idea. Gnomon, sundial. Seeing so many sundials without stumbling across the one pictured in the book hadn't made sense. The odds were against it. Natalie had realized that perhaps the clue wasn't a particular sundial, but *sundials in general*. And maybe, just maybe, Alex had turned his picture clue into a word puzzle. With the aid of the thesaurus, Natalie wrote down synonyms for all of the clues, then put each word onto its own scrap of paper. If it was a word game, then maybe the order of the words, a combination of words, would be the answer.

Over an hour later she had discovered that combining three clues, *gnomon*, *clay* and *door*, produced nomenclator.

Shaking her head in disbelief, Natalie grabbed the dictionary before any more doubts surfaced. She summarized the definition in real terms: a nomenclator was a person who invented names for or gave names to things, such as scientific classifications. *A system of names*.

Natalie set the dictionary aside, chewing the end of her pen as she thought about what she had learned. A system of names, a person who classifies. Where would one use such a system? she asked herself, then quickly jotted down two possibilities. Museums. Libraries.

Excited again, she grabbed her list of Oxford clues. Deleting what had already been used, Natalie found herself left with three items. Animals, stars and the round table. She added museums and libraries. Writing furiously, she joined the words in every possible combination, having realized she was no longer playing a word game, but a guessing game. In less than ten minutes she had three promising variations.

First of all, animals—alive—could be found in a zoo, but Oxford didn't boast one. Animals—dead—could be found in museums, and she found the names of two that might have natural history exhibits. Libraries were also sources for organized animal studies, and she put down the names of a couple of the public ones as options.

Next Natalie considered the starry sky. A planetarium or observatory would be the logical place to look, but Natalie couldn't find either listed in the guidebooks. Natalie checked the list of museums, adding a couple to her list of options.

Finally she considered the round table, then crossed it out. For the time being, Natalie couldn't seem to connect it to anything she had so far discovered. Perhaps its significance would become clear after she had more information.

Natalie was anxious to call Neil Stanhope in New York to run her theories by him. If her guesses were correct, he would point her in the right direction, saving her both time and wasted effort. *If her guesses were correct,* she reminded herself, the rush of adrenalin she'd felt at the initial discovery fading somewhat under the onslaught of uncertainty.

But right or wrong, Natalie was becoming convinced of one thing. Alex had a devious mind, and if the rest of the puzzle was as convoluted as the Oxford section, then she had her work cut out for her.

She was just reaching for the telephone to call Stanhope when it rang. No one knew she was here, not even

Liz, but she recovered quickly, curiosity getting the better of her as she picked up the instrument.

"Mr. Garrick called to say he would be delayed half an hour for dinner," the hotel operator told her. Message delivered, the connection was cut, leaving her alone with a pulse that had jumped off the scale.

6

STANHOPE LISTENED carefully, desperately searching for an explanation for Garrick's behavior.

There was none.

And for now he couldn't think what to tell Murdoch, except to keep a close eye on Natalie Tracy.

With hands that shook, he cradled the receiver and opened the bottom drawer of his desk. Pulling out the bottle and glass, he poured a double measure of whiskey and returned the bottle to the drawer. It took discipline not to gulp the liquor, and Stanhope concentrated on taking small sips as he reviewed the new information.

Garrick was stalking the Tracy woman, alternately shadowing and surprising her. She hadn't been out of his sight all day, making the job of Stanhope's accomplice that much more difficult. Not only was he having trouble keeping up with her, he was in danger of tripping over Garrick at any moment.

And according to the information from the room clerk, she was meeting him for dinner.

Why?

Did Garrick have a reason of his own for not wanting the puzzle solved? Although Stanhope couldn't understand why, it was consistent with Garrick's protest over the test. More importantly, why didn't Garrick simply tamper with a few of the clues and prevent her from finishing without exposing himself? In Oxford, for example, he could do something about that exhibit in the museum, deface it in such a way they'd have to withdraw it from view—and without that, she'd be lost. It wouldn't be easy, Stanhope granted, but then, since he didn't know why Garrick might want to stop her, he couldn't know what risks he'd be willing to take.

Stanhope had considered doing something along those lines himself, until he discovered how closely his conversations with Natalie would be monitored. The vice president expected progress reports, and a lack of progress due to an absence of clues would stick out like a sore thumb.

Sweat broke out across his brow as Stanhope considered another possibility. *Was Garrick helping her?* If so, why didn't they just work together instead of playing this hide-and-seek game all day. If he was helping, then something would have to be done. Soon, before they got too close to the end.

Waiting was never easy, particularly when you didn't know what you were waiting for. And Stanhope had never been a patient man.

That was why he was in this mess. He hadn't been able to wait to earn the reward he knew he deserved, so he had just taken it.

Reaching down into the drawer for the bottle, he settled back to wait for Natalie's call. Perhaps when she told him about her close brush with the Land-Rover, he would feel better.

Too late, he wished they had taken the opportunity to get rid of her that morning. The way things were going, it might have made things easier all around.

And who knows? Garrick might even agree.

NATALIE SMOOTHED THE SKIRT over her hips with hands that were remarkably steady, then turned to check her appearance in the full-length mirror. Satisfied that makeup, hair and clothing were in order, she let out a breath of relief. The butterflies that had been fluttering madly in her tummy for the past couple of hours subsided to occasional quivers of anticipation.

With a sense of feminine pleasure she congratulated herself on her new purchase. The dress was the perfect choice for an evening out in the cool, English springtime, the soft cashmere knit subtly hinting at the curves beneath. The natural color of the wool was a quiet complement to the rich auburn waves that fell freely about her shoulders.

Grinning at her reflection in the bathroom mirror, Natalie gave up pretending she was merely excited by the puzzle. Her earlier resolution to ignore Alex and concentrate solely on the game had faded with the afternoon sunshine. It was no longer a matter of what came first or second. Why couldn't she have both?

Besides, it was only one evening. Only dinner, for heaven's sake! It wasn't as though she was sacrificing her professional integrity for a free meal. She could accomplish no more on the puzzle tonight, and there was nothing in the rules that said she couldn't enjoy herself.

Magic, he'd said. She wanted to believe he had meant it, wanted to explore for herself the source of the electricity that flashed between them.

The key was to keep Alex, the man, apart from Alexander Garrick, a.k.a. Gregory Lewis, the creator of the treasure hunt. And Alex the man fascinated her far more than any man she'd ever met. Something unfamiliar inside Natalie drove her to learn more about him.

It was only dinner, she reminded herself once again. *Would that be enough?*

It would have to be. After tomorrow she would most likely be leaving Oxford, and therefore leaving Alex. Dinner was all she could afford. Anything more was inconceivable. She was attracted to him, but brief, sexual flings were definitely not her style.

Wandering back into the bedroom, Natalie took a moment to tidy the reference books and leaflets strewn about the room into a neat pile. Tucking a couple that she might need the next day into her shoulder bag, Natalie put the rest into her suitcase and pulled the zipper closed. Her telephone conversation with Neil Stanhope had confirmed her hunch, and she hoped to finish the Oxford stage of the puzzle tomorrow. Professionally speaking, she had made definitive progress, and the adrenaline rush brought on by this first victory left her euphoric.

Tomorrow she would discover if she really knew what she was doing, or if that first success was merely a case of blind luck.

Glancing at her watch, she saw she had enough time to check in with Liz. As she dialed the number, Natalie wondered how she would get through the twenty minutes before Alex was due if her friend wasn't available. Fortunately, Liz's cheerful voice at the other end of the line saved her.

"Mrs. Wilkins lost her watch. Twice. I think she's testing me."

"Did you find it?" Natalie asked, surprised at the tug of envy that had popped out of nowhere. Mrs. Wilkins had been her personal client for so long that Natalie regarded her as family.

"The first time I did." Liz regaled Natalie with the details of her first exposure to the problem of the missing watch game. From the sound of it, Liz had thoroughly enjoyed herself, and Natalie giggled at Liz's blow-by-blow description of the event.

"She called again this morning. I was just on my way over to her house."

Natalie was glad that Liz had taken Mrs. Wilkins's case instead of assigning it to one of the regular investigative staff. The idea of having Liz as a full partner was becoming more and more attractive.

"Lots of luck," Natalie said, grinning to herself at the image of Mrs. Wilkins deliberately hiding her watch.

"If things get too busy around here, I'll pick up one of those cheap, fashion watches at the drugstore and send it over," Liz joked. "Do you think she'd like a pink or a purple band?"

Natalie let that pass, silently commending Liz for a brilliant idea. While pink and purple bands wouldn't compare with the gold ones Mrs. Wilkins usually favored, she would at least know she hadn't been forgotten. Natalie pressed on to more general topics. "Anything else going on I should know about?"

"You've only been gone three days, Nat."

"It seems like a century," she murmured, thinking of all that had happened. Had there ever been a time when she hadn't known Alex?

"What about that author guy, er, something Garrick?"

"Alex." Natalie supplied his name before she could stop herself, then mentally kicked her shin fifteen times.

"Well?"

"Well, nothing!" Natalie managed to get out. "He just showed me around a little yesterday."

"Wow!" Liz was impressed. Wow was her ultimate exclamation. "Are those eyes for real, or something the photographer threw in for free?"

"They're real. But you'd better quit drooling, Liz," Natalie warned, "or I'll tell Darrin you were looking at another man."

"Darrin won't mind as long as I keep the Atlantic Ocean between me and your Alex."

"He's not my Alex," Natalie insisted, unexpectedly flustered by Liz's assumption.

"We'll see, Boss," Liz replied coolly. "We'll see."

Natalie chose to ignore her, letting the dare slide by as she reported on her progress with the puzzle. Apparently getting the hint, Liz briefly outlined progress on a couple of the more important, ongoing cases, then said, "I decided to add a temporary secretary to the office staff. Things were getting a little hairy. I guess you do more around here than I thought."

"I'm glad you miss me."

"I didn't say I missed you. I just said—"

Natalie cut her off before the conversation could deteriorate any further. "Give my best to Darrin."

"I will." Even across the thousands of miles that separated them, Natalie could easily tell Liz's tone had changed from teasing to dreamy.

"And his mother," Natalie couldn't help adding.

"If I must," Liz moaned.

Promising to call the next day, Natalie replaced the receiver. Boston, the agency and Mrs. Wilkins seemed a lifetime away. But her adventure would end—and so would her involvement with Alex Garrick.

"I NEVER ACTUALLY SAID I'd go to dinner with you."

"Then why are you here?"

"I'm hungry."

"You look pretty good for a hungry woman."

"Pretty good?" she repeated, arresting the movement of her fork momentarily before letting it continue its journey to her mouth. Natalie took her time, enjoying the delicately seasoned salmon mousse while she looked forward to the entrée. "'Pretty good' sounds like you've been watching too much American television."

"I read a lot," Alex confessed with a smile, the flash of white teeth sending shivers down her spine. Dressed in a dark suit and silk tie, he was the sexiest man she'd ever seen. His rugged features were too harsh to be considered handsome, but she was well aware that other women in the restaurant were staring at Alex with the same fascination she was trying hard to conceal.

"What if I said you were lovely?"

"I'd blush," she admitted, then proceeded to do so. The rush of bright color to her cheeks was an adolescent reaction she'd never outgrown, and Natalie took a healthy gulp of wine in a bid for instant relief.

His eyes commanded her attention, the humor replaced by something hot and provocative. In a low, husky tone, he murmured, "Then I'd better not tell you the way that dress clings to your body leaves me breathless."

Natalie choked on the wine, the heat pulsing through her body and deepening the color in her face. Pressing a napkin to her lips, she tried desperately to recover.

Easing back in his chair, Alex contemplated the flustered woman across the table. From the moment he'd watched her descend the stairs into the hotel lobby, it had been a battle to keep his hands off her.

Slowly, he'd promised himself . . . promised her. It would happen. She would come to him with her eyes open, not because she was seduced by the electricity between them, but because she wanted him as desperately as he wanted her.

"Did you . . . ?" she began in a high-pitched squeak, then cleared her throat and tried again. "Did you follow me all afternoon?"

"Yes."

"You shouldn't have."

"Why not?" he asked mildly.

Natalie didn't have an answer and could hardly pretend that she minded. "I didn't see you."

"You weren't looking."

Natalie conceded the point, resolving to dump her yellow jacket the next day. "You knew I wouldn't go to The Black Horse."

"I guessed," he said, the tone of his voice more amused than reproachful.

As the waiter served the mouth-watering entrée and an assortment of fresh vegetables, Alex quirked an eyebrow and asked, "Truce?"

"Truce."

Natalie changed the subject. Many times. Between bites and with much prompting from Alex, she talked about her agency in Boston, her life there and her impressions of England so far. Over coffee she heard the story—exaggerated, she was convinced—of Alex's first novel. She concluded that Alex had fought long and hard just to get someone in the publishing trade to read his book. It gave Natalie a sense of comradeship to know they had both worked to achieve success.

The one thing he didn't ask surprised her. He didn't ask about the treasure hunt. To be fair, Natalie wanted to credit his reticence to Rule #1. But an unwanted suspicion gnawed at her, cautioning against giving up too much too soon. Thus far he'd given her little reason to trust him.

"I've been meaning to ask about when you were in the village. Did you mention Gregory Lewis?"

"Your pen name for the treasure book? No, I didn't think anyone would know it," she said easily. "Not yet, anyway."

Alex smiled congenially, relieved that she hadn't given away his secret. The last thing he needed was to have that particular link exposed. When the waiter brought the cognac and coffee he'd ordered, Alex proceeded to tell her the history of her hotel.

Natalie was entertained, but not fooled for a second. Alex had something to hide, and it involved his pseudonym. But until she could figure out if it had any bearing on her own project, she decided to leave it alone. Time was precious.

"What are you working on now?" she asked, remembering the mess she'd seen on his desk.

"What makes you think I'm working on anything?" he countered, his eyes glinting mischievously over the rim of the snifter.

Natalie flushed again under his persistent gaze, then dropped her eyes to concentrate on the pattern she was drawing on the white linen cloth with the dessert spoon.

"If you're not, then you need a better filing system," she teased, still not daring to look up. "Your desk looked like a bomb had exploded over it and you couldn't be bothered to sort out the rubble."

"I'm surprised you noticed," he murmured, catching her fingers with his own, forcing them to cease their nervous movements. Slipping his strong fingers into the gaps between her own, he firmly joined their hands with a movement that was almost too intimate to bear. "I should have apologized then for bringing you into that chaos. But I was preoccupied. . . ."

"Preoccupied?" She gulped in air, willing herself to ignore the tantalizing warmth generated by his palm.

"Yes, preoccupied," he echoed, dropping his voice to a seductive murmur. "I was watching the reflection of the fire in your hair, and thinking how much I wanted to bury my face in its soft waves."

Natalie jerked her hand from his grasp; she didn't want him to detect the trembling that had overtaken her. It had to be the wine they'd shared at dinner, she decided. Alex's words certainly hadn't surprised her. She had been expecting something from him all evening. Whether or not he was sincere wasn't the point.

It was only supposed to be dinner! Nothing more . . . certainly not this exciting roller coaster that soared and plunged without warning! She had wanted to explore the electricity between them, but had pretended it was only an intellectual exercise. Now she was breathless with an incredible yearning, an almost overwhelming attraction that threatened to rage out of control . . . at the very least, out of *her* control!

Meeting his eyes, Natalie was startled to realize that he knew precisely what she was feeling, that he had deliberately provoked her response and was enjoying watching her fight the erotic sensations that coursed through her body.

"No," she said firmly, holding his gaze with her own, as if by sheer willpower she could regain control of the situation.

"No?"

"No," Natalie repeated, clenching her teeth with almost painful determination. "I won't let you seduce me."

At that his eyebrows rose, and Natalie had the impression he was astonished by her statement.

"Seduction implies a certain unwillingness by one of the participants. That's not my intention," he said coolly.

"I don't understand," she lied, wishing the floor would just open and swallow her.

"You'll come to me because you want to. Not because *I* want you to."

Natalie shook her head in disbelief. Nothing in her life had prepared her for Alex's frank remarks. "I can't. I won't."

"What about last night?" he asked. "I could have sworn you felt differently. You as much as admitted you did at lunch today."

"So I changed my mind." It was useless to deny what she had already more or less confessed. She tried another tactic—evasion.

"Oh?"

"I was jet-lagged. Tired. Things kind of got out of control." She smiled apologetically. "I don't have time to pursue a...relationship." Weak, Natalie, very weak, she scolded herself. But it was the best she could do under the circumstances. After tonight she would most likely be leaving Oxford and would never see Alex again. *And one night wouldn't be enough. One night with Alex could never be enough.*

What was almost as important, she still didn't know if his motives were related to the puzzle, or if he simply wanted to share an erotic experience with a woman he would probably never run into again.

"Fine. It's your choice, Natalie. It will always be your choice. I'll accept nothing less."

"And that means . . . ?"

"That means I'm taking you back to your room. You must be tired." Signaling to the waiter for the bill, Alex struggled to remain indifferent to Natalie's presence, to the scent of her perfume, to her trembling fingers. Maintaining this delicate balance between satisfying an immediate lust and enjoying a continued passion was playing havoc with his body.

He would give her another night to think about them. Alone, without any pressure, she might come to her senses.

And he'd spend the days persuading her that the puzzle shouldn't come between them, though things might get a little tricky, especially since she would soon be leaving Oxford.

Alex had been more than a little surprised to learn that. Nothing he'd observed so far had suggested Natalie had made significant progress, yet she had told the hotel's receptionist she would probably be leaving the next afternoon or evening.

He had no choice but to follow her.

SHE SHOULD HAVE been relieved.

Ten minutes after leaving the restaurant, Natalie was in her room alone. Alex had escorted her to the hotel and said good-night under the watchful eye of the night porter.

Would he follow her tomorrow?

Why should he? she countered. He hadn't even kissed her. Preparing for bed, she tried to think about the puzzle and what she needed to accomplish the next day, but couldn't get Alex out of her mind. Was there more to his interest than personal attraction? She didn't know and couldn't come up with any reasons he'd want to keep such close track of her progress. To be sure, he objected to the test in principle, but there was nothing to be gained from stopping her.

Or was there?

The question startled Natalie, and apprehension tightened the knot in her stomach.

She asked the question again. *What would he have to gain by stopping me?* Blaming her overactive imagination on the lateness of the hour, she pushed aside the disagreeable thoughts and slipped between the cool sheets.

All he'd done was follow her. Was that such a bad thing? Not if all he wanted was to see her again, she argued with herself.

But she didn't win the argument.

7

NATALIE LOOKED over her shoulder again.

Alex wasn't following her.

But he seemed to be the only one in town who wasn't. A camera-rich flock of Japanese tourists had been dogging her steps after waylaying her for directions. She knew no more than they did about the layout of Oxford, but was the only one with a map, and the group seemed to respect her foresight in buying one.

And while Natalie admitted her oriental fan club would provide excellent cover for almost anyone trying to follow her, Alex was one man who would stand out in this crowd. His blond hair and imposing height would be instantly noticeable, so Natalie continued her trek across town, assured that no one following her spoke the Queen's English.

Straightening his cramped legs, Alex pulled the peak of his cloth cap over his eyes. Hiding an extra six inches of height in this crowd was no mean feat, and his duck-legged gait was beginning to draw curious stares from his newfound Japanese buddies.

They were approaching the end of Broad Street, and Alex decided his cover was about to disappear. Responding entirely to instinct, he dodged into an open doorway, counted to ten, then gave in to the urge to peer out. They had disappeared, all of them. But there was only one place where they could have gone: The Museum of the History of Science.

It made sense—for Natalie, at least. He wasn't so sure about her companions. Deciding to take a new tack, Alex headed across the street to The White Horse. The tiny pub served a good cup of coffee, and Alex claimed a window table, settling down to wait in comfort.

He wished he could have taken the chance of following her inside the museum. He'd like to watch her work, get an idea of how she thought as she worked her way through the puzzle. She seemed to be stumbling along . . . in the right direction, to be sure, but still missing the essence of the clue. Natalie was in the wrong museum, but Alex was impressed by the fact she'd made it that far.

It was the wrong museum, Natalie decided. There were instruments of indeterminate age and use as well as recognizable prototypes of modern scientific equipment. But none of them suggested animals, even less a round table. Nor did any exhibit offer a clear connection to stars. This was definitely the wrong place. But years of training prevented her from leaving immediately. She systematically checked every room and passageway, albeit at a pace that challenged all visitors' speed records.

Two other museums remained on her list, and Natalie was undecided whether to stop for coffee before or after the next one. The pub across the road looked welcoming, and the full, English breakfast she'd eaten that morning was no longer sustaining her. The camera crowd, however, clicked to a stop on her heels, breathless from her speedy tour and eager for more of the same. With a sigh, Natalie signaled Forward Ho with a flick of her wrist, headed down the street and into a narrow lane.

One more dusty museum, then she'd stop. She would have to find a bigger pub, though, if it was to hold her entire party.

NATALIE STUDIED THE EXHIBIT from all angles, neither daring to believe she'd found it nor quite sure what she'd found.

Pleiades—the Seven Sisters, a cluster of stars in the constellation Taurus. An astronomy exhibit in the lobby of a natural history museum.

Natalie had seen multiple examples of stuffed animals and skeletal displays, everything from dodo birds to hamsters. Now she was seeing stars. The display didn't belong in a natural history museum.

Munching what might or might not be a lamb pita sandwich from a nearby kebab van, Natalie sat on the lawn in front of the Pitt Rivers Museum and examined her conclusions. If she was right, two of the last three clues had been successfully dealt with. Animals could point to this museum, and stars could indicate the Pleiades exhibit.

But the round table continued to worry her. Stuffing the sandwich wrapper into a nearby bin, Natalie hiked over to the third museum on her list. Her Japanese tourists had opted for an open-top bus tour of the city, leaving Natalie alone with her stars and furry animals.

She no longer bothered to check over her shoulder for Alex. He had either lost interest or had better things to do than traipse around Oxford all day.

Either way she was alone.

STANHOPE BEGAN TO SWEAT the second his secretary signaled the call. "You've made an excellent beginning, Miss Tracy." Keeping his voice cheerful and steady wasn't really a problem. He'd had a lot of practice at that lately.

Natalie Tracy was working too fast, much faster than he'd dreamed. And Oxford was one of the trickiest segments. Frantically Stanhope tried to figure what to do, how to retard her pace. But he couldn't afford to slow her down with misinformation. It would be too easy to get caught; there were too many other people in the office involved with the puzzle. Besides, Garrick must be helping her. That was the only explanation for her early success. And if that was true, nothing he did would stop her.

Almost nothing.

"The Pleiades or Seven Sisters is the correct clue," he finally added, setting aside his alarm. "Congratulations."

"But I'm really not sure what it means."

"You know enough."

"And the round table?" Natalie still hadn't discovered where it fitted into the puzzle, much less what it had to with Oxford. As far as she was concerned, that was almost as bad as having a clue with no meaning.

"No reason to stay in Oxford," he continued and directed her to Edinburgh—the site of the next set of clues. Gently replacing the receiver, Neil Stanhope tried to appear as though nothing was wrong; to be sure, he saw a faint tremble in his hand when he picked up his pen to sign the letters his secretary brought into his office. He forced himself to wait until lunchtime to tackle the problem of Natalie Tracy.

Sitting alone in a corner booth of his favorite restaurant, Stanhope considered the steps that had already been taken. The brush with the Land-Rover hadn't been anything more than an attempt to frighten her. An injury would have attracted too much attention, but a little scare should have slowed her down. Not only had she escaped injury, the Tracy woman hadn't even mentioned the incident.

And while Stanhope hadn't wanted her to connect the accident with the treasure hunt, he had hoped she would become more cautious. Instead, she was already finished with Oxford and on her way to Edinburgh. A stronger deterrent was needed.

Garrick or no Garrick, she had to be stopped.

SHE'D FINISHED with Oxford.

Alex watched her go into the Pitt Rivers Museum for the second time, then followed her back to the hotel after a brief detour to another museum. If he read the signs right, she was preparing to leave.

Sliding from behind the pillar in the lobby, Alex crossed to the reception desk and skillfully extracted Natalie's travel plans from the clerk. Checking his watch, he found he had more than enough time to return home to pack a suitcase.

The night train to Edinburgh didn't leave until after midnight, and he intended to be on it. Alex pulled his car into the late-afternoon traffic, heading for the railway station. Although the hotel clerk had offered to make his reservation, Alex did it himself. It wouldn't help if Natalie accidentally discovered his plans and changed her own.

Besides, Natalie was traveling second class. They'd never get any privacy anywhere outside his first-class compartment.

TOO LATE, Natalie discovered the difference between first- and standard-class sleeper accommodations. She didn't mind sharing a cabin with a total stranger, although it had taken her by surprise when the other woman had boarded the train in Banbury and proceeded to overwhelm Natalie with her excitement about her travel plans.

Natalie had hoped to spend the night sleeping. Instead, she fled the tiny cabin in search of a quieter corner. The dining car proved to be her best alternative. She was congratulating herself on her escape, wondering how long she would have to stay away for her roommate to fall asleep, when the familiar voice interrupted.

"I'd join you if there was room." Alex glanced innocently about the overcrowded dining car as if seeking a vacant chair, flashing a winning smile at her table companions when it became obvious there wasn't a seat to be found.

Smothering the fireball of excitement that shot through her bloodstream beneath a blanket of indifference, Natalie smiled coolly. "I'd invite you to my place, but my roomie might object."

"Roomie?" Alex paused only a few seconds before asking for clarification, hesitant about being tricked into another Dick Tracy dialogue.

"Yes, roomie. As in roommate, cohabitant of the cabin, the perfect stranger asleep in the top bunk."

"Oh. Roomie."

"Nobody warned me about her. She just kind of appeared."

"That happens," he commiserated.

"To me more than most, I think." And when Alex nodded sagely in agreement, Natalie grinned. Unexpected roommates were among the least startling of the surprises Natalie had experienced in England.

"We could always go to my compartment," he suggested, with just the hint of a leer thrown in for entertainment value to the three people who were sharing Natalie's small table.

"Probably not." She smiled sweetly, virtue intact, while she sensed her companions waiting breathlessly for the next installment.

"Then perhaps a compromise. The Pullman car." Alex was leaning over the table, trying to limit their audience to the three other travellers at the table. But a quick glance around them suggested there was avid interest in their conversation. It was time for a strategic change of scenery.

"How do I get past the dragon at the gate?" Natalie, like everyone else in the dining car, was fully aware of the plush lounge just a few steps away. The fact that it was limited to first-class passengers was a shame, and not for the first time Natalie wished she'd known to book a first-class ticket. What were expense accounts for, if not to take advantage of the occasional perk!

Alex grinned. "Trust me."

"Trust you?" Natalie shook her head, but stood up and took the hand he held out to her. "Trust you? You've got to be kidding!"

"Someday, Natalie," he breathed into her ear. "Someday."

Pretending she hadn't heard the whispered promise, Natalie did her best to conceal the shudder that betrayed her lack of indifference and led the way.

At the doorway to the first-class section, Alex drew ahead and spoke quietly with the porter. Natalie ignored the exchange, wishing she had a scotch to pour over the butterflies in her stomach. Congratulating herself on having done her homework on the Edin-

burgh part of *The Quest* earlier that evening, she waited
for the end of the exchange. While his sudden appearance was no immediate threat to her progress, Natalie
swore to herself that after this she could no longer spend
time with him.

Until the puzzle was solved, that is. Then it would
be up to Alex.

Remembering the puzzle put things back into perspective, and the fiery excitement of the last few moments died.

Whatever his motives, Natalie could no longer consider herself safe in his company. A personal or professional threat . . . it didn't matter which. One was just as
destructive as the other, and she was determined to
survive with her integrity and emotions intact.

Tomorrow in Edinburgh she'd lose him. She had no
choice.

In the meantime she would enjoy his company. *What
harm could there be in that?*

Given permission to pass, they negotiated the narrow hallway between the cars and followed the porter
through a final doorway. Alex laid his palm just above
her hip and steadied Natalie as they passed through into
the Pullman car, only dropping the hand when they
were seated. Natalie immediately missed the comfortable intimacy of his palm, then admonished herself for
exaggerating what was no more than a common courtesy.

So why was this the first time she'd enjoyed simple
courtesy so thoroughly?

The noise level was dramatically lower here, and
Natalie could now enjoy the passing light show from a
window seat. The lounge was sparsely populated, and
the white-coated waiter soon brought them cognac in

tiny snifters. Relieved to be away from the noisy dining car, Natalie relaxed in the comfortable armchair and nibbled at the selection of cheeses Alex had ordered.

Sprawled comfortably on the plush bench seat across from her, Alex tipped his glass in her direction. "May I offer my congratulations?"

"Not without breaking Rule #1." Talking with Alex was fun, and she approached the verbal duel with a sense of reckless enjoyment.

"Then what shall we drink to?" he countered, his eyes bright with unmistakable suggestion.

Natalie had to force herself to breathe evenly. "To a white Christmas." That should change the subject! She snuggled deeper into the chair, grateful for the burning liquid that stung her nerve endings before lulling them into a deep sense of contentment.

"You plan ahead," was his only comment as he raised his glass, then downed a large portion of the fiery spirit.

"Just the important stuff," she retorted.

"Like where you'll be sleeping tonight?" he asked, without missing a beat, grinning at the sudden blush that covered her face.

Sleeping was the last thing on her mind. But Natalie rallied, determined to win this war of words, knowing she was fighting for more than a few points on an invisible scoreboard.

"I thought that was all settled." It was hard to decide what he was really thinking behind those shadowed eyes. Was he teasing her, or did he assume there was really a question as to where she would spend the remainder of the night.

After all, wasn't this the same man who had left her the night before without even a kiss?

"You didn't kiss me last night," Alex said.

Natalie tried very hard not to spill the remaining cognac, brushing a few, stray drops from her slacks as she leaned forward to place the glass very carefully on the table.

"You didn't ask," she pointed out prosaically. "About kissing me, that is."

"And I'm not asking now," he said mildly, signaling the waiter for another round. "Just pointing out a fact."

It wasn't supposed to hurt, she reminded herself. They were just joking around, playing with words. *Just because you want him more than anything you've ever wanted in your life, he shouldn't have the power to hurt.*

But saying it was one thing, believing it another.

"Then what's your beef?" In her attempt to sidestep the emotional turmoil caused by his teasing denial, Natalie returned to their verbal tangle.

"Beef?" he asked.

"No beef on this train, sir," the waiter interjected. "We're only serving lamb or fresh salmon tonight. And the kitchen will be closed in ten minutes." He set the new glasses on the table and removed the pair of empty ones, then waited stoically for further instructions.

Natalie giggled at Alex's lost expression, not at all chastised by the waiter's disapproving glare. "No, thank you, Alex. I'll just finish this drink before retiring," she said innocently. "But if you're hungry..."

"I'm not hungry!" he thundered, causing the waiter to jump, as well as attracting the interest of an elderly couple a few tables away. Their raised eyebrows showed Alex precisely what they thought of his outburst. It was a subtle reminder that a proper English gentleman would never allow himself to be goaded into displaying more than mild annoyance—no matter what the provocation.

"Very good, sir," the waiter said hurriedly, stepping away from their table and scurrying toward the bar at the other end of the car.

Thoroughly enjoying her easy victory, Natalie grinned at Alex, daring him to ask again.

Alex buried his curiosity about the strange phrase she had used. For a reason he couldn't fathom, he admired her ability to talk in riddles.

They had been talking of more important matters, and it was time to return to them. "We were talking about kissing."

"No, we weren't," she said easily. "We were talking about *not* kissing."

"Let's not get technical," he chided. Then, before she had a chance to gloat, he added, "Let's go to my compartment." Extending his hand across the table, he dared Natalie to take it.

She didn't—a fact that surprised neither of them.

He wasn't playing any longer, his intent was real. Burning under the fiery promise of his gaze, Natalie slowly shook her head. Conscious that in ignoring the rush of excitement that must surely be showing just as clearly in her own eyes, she knew she was denying herself the one thing she wanted most.

Flinging her gaze about, as if there might be salvation just a few feet away, Natalie desperately sought an escape from Alex . . . from the almost overwhelming need to take his hand and go with him, whatever the consequences.

But it was Alex who saved her. He withdrew his hand and the offer disappeared, leaving Natalie breathless at the thought of what might have been.

Alex could almost see the tension lift from her shoulders. "It's a small compartment, anyway," he admitted, enjoying the tentative return of her smile.

"It's probably for the best," Natalie assured him. "Would you be man enough to tell my roommate I wouldn't be coming home tonight?"

"Probably not," he responded, cheerfully admitting his cowardice.

"Then I should probably get back there before she reports me missing." She was genuinely relieved to see his smile return, although the calculating gaze did nothing to restore her calm.

"How much longer are you going to keep running away?" he asked idly.

"I haven't been running away," she stated primly. "I've been working and—"

"And making me work for every minute we spend together," he finished.

"You can always stop." Natalie stood up, half afraid he wouldn't take her suggestion and half afraid he would. Grasping the edge of the table to keep her balance against the unfamiliar movement of the train, she waited breathlessly for his answer.

"Is that what you want?" he asked, rising to offer her his hand.

Natalie stared at his hand for the second time that night, then placed her own in the center of his palm. A measure of trust, that was all she was giving. But it was a beginning, and she took comfort in the warmth of his flesh.

"No, Alex," she admitted softly, "but it's most likely what I *should* want." And she raised her eyes to meet his, pleading for his understanding.

To her surprise, that was precisely what she got.

"Perhaps you worry too much about what you should want and do, Natalie."

"Yes."

He studied her face for a long moment, then came to a decision. Drawing her close, Alex slipped an arm around her shoulders and began the journey back to her compartment. *Slowly*, he reminded himself as they walked silently through the narrow corridors and over the noisy platforms between the carriages. *Slowly*.

It didn't surprise Natalie that Alex knew precisely where her sleeping compartment was located. Had she any reason to expect less from him? Wordlessly she ducked away from the protective warmth of his arm and turned, pressing her face against the cool glass as she looked onto a station platform. They had stopped, and she hadn't even noticed the absence of movement.

Maybe if she just ignored him, he would go away. But she knew Alex would leave only when he was ready, not before. Natalie wrapped her fingers tightly around the brass fittings at the base of the window, knowing he was watching her, wishing for something she couldn't define. She heard the whistle blast the warning of their impending departure, watched as the station was slowly left behind.

Alex rested his palm on the back of her neck, resolutely drawing her attention from the moving train, his fingers lightly rubbing the soft skin hidden from sight by the heavy, silken waves. But she didn't turn to him.

Trust. That was what it was all about. Trust and confidence. When Natalie trusted him, when she was confident of his motives and intentions, then she would come to him freely. Alex knew this, but was still tortured by each hour that passed without her.

The outcome of this game he was playing was steadily gaining importance, and while he wasn't quite sure about its meaning, he knew enough to guard against failure. Besides, he was no longer certain it was just a game.

But for now he had to taste her lips again. The need to bury his tongue in the moist warmth of her sweet mouth was almost crushing, and he could deny himself no longer. He flexed the fingers at her neck, then slid his hand across to tug at her shoulder.

At first Natalie resisted. But Alex was persistent, gently forcing her to turn and face him. She knew he was going to kiss her. It was what she had been waiting for. But she was unprepared for the wave of disappointment that followed the realization that a kiss would be all they shared. Otherwise he wouldn't have brought her back to her cabin, to her roommate.

"Open your mouth," he whispered against her lips, pressing the length of his body against hers, crushing her against the windows and holding them both steady against the train's movement.

Natalie gasped, and her involuntary response allowed him what he wanted. Growling his pleasure, Alex pushed his tongue past her teeth and into the tender softness of her mouth. He devoured her without preliminaries, hungrily taking what he wanted, challenging her to respond. Tangling his fingers in the long waves of her hair, he held her captive for his assault, using only the slightest pressure to change the angle of her mouth for a deeper kiss, another taste.

Natalie gave...willingly, passionately. Dragging up her hands to grasp his shoulders, she opened herself to his lead, imitating the incredibly erotic movements of his tongue, drawing her own under and along his, teasing the roof of his mouth, exploring the smooth teeth that playfully bit back at her.

The intimate thrust of his hips startled her. Suddenly it was more than a kiss, and she couldn't remember why it was wrong. Twisting away from his demanding mouth only gave him new territory to explore, and Alex enthusiastically traced the curve of her ear. Natalie nearly fainted as this new sensation gave birth to a series of tremors that began at the base of her spine and raced up and down at dizzying speeds.

But it was his whispered promise of the delights to come that finally penetrated her consciousness and dragged her back to the reality of a windy corridor on a racing train.

As she tried to decipher his whispers with her befuddled brain, her eyes glimpsed a short man at the far end of the car.

Her chest heaving, Natalie used the same hands to push Alex away that had just moments before been clinging to him. Not too far away, just far enough to be able to breathe without inhaling the scent of his old-fashioned, minty after-shave. Critical inches away from the broad, masculine chest that had nearly crushed her resistance.

His eyes held an invitation—one that stole her breath and nearly made her forget why she'd pushed him away in the first place.

"There was a man watching," She jerked her head at where the man had been, but Alex did no more than glance carelessly in the direction she indicated.

Leaning negligently against the paneled door of her compartment, he waited for her to compose herself. She was unnerved by the intensity of what they had just shared. He was, too, but that was the last thing he wanted her to know. To admit his own need for her would be to admit a weakness . . . to lose control, and Alex wasn't prepared to make that sacrifice.

Not for any woman.

The man she'd seen didn't worry him. While the sight of a man kissing a woman certainly wasn't unusual enough to attract crowds, the occasional voyeur might find it interesting. All the same, Alex didn't like the thought of exposing Natalie to curious onlookers, and chastised himself for forgetting where they were.

But she'd made it too easy to forget. The taste and feel of her sweet mouth, the softness of her breasts against his chest . . . Alex tried to repress the shudder that ripped through him, disguising the passionate response with an exaggerated flex of seemingly stiff shoulder muscles. He had to go before he dragged her back into his embrace and then to his bed.

"Don't worry about anyone watching. There wasn't anything to see." But there might have been. Just being near her made him forget about the rest of the world.

She nodded, wishing he would leave. Kissing Alex had been too good, too exciting. She had to get away, back to a place where she could think about her job, her life and her runaway emotions. But with him standing there, all she could think about was the shattering impact of his lips against hers.

Long moments passed and neither of them made a move. Something had changed between them, and it seemed as though neither wanted to break the tenuous link. Only the slam of a door broke the mood.

"Good night, Alex," Natalie whispered. *Goodbye*, she added silently.

"Sleep well." So formal, he thought. So wrong. There shouldn't be scenes like this between them. Instead they should be undressing and touching, whispering words of passion and excitement, learning to please and be pleased.

She waited until he pulled himself away from the door, then put her hand out to slide it open.

"And Natalie . . ."

"Yes?"

"The next time I kiss you, it won't be in a public place."

It was a promise that Alex intended to keep. This time he would leave her to sleep alone. This one, last time.

MURDOCH HEARD the door slide shut, but stayed in the shadows for a few moments longer, cursing his rotten luck.

For starters, the woman had disappeared into the first-class section with the writer, although why he was on the train was unknown. That was something he'd have to find out and soon. Only after spending hours waiting for them in the dining car had he been rewarded when they returned.

The little scene he'd interrupted in the corridor wouldn't make Stanhope happy at all. What if Garrick was helping the Tracy woman? That could really be a bigger problem than the one they already had. But he shrugged it aside, knowing that where there was a solution for one, there was a solution for the other.

A joint accident? He'd check with Stanhope, just in case. Maybe the other little mishap he'd planned wouldn't be enough now.

Besides, she'd seen him now, and that added a level of risk that had been virtually absent until now.

He had to admit, though, it made the entire undertaking more exciting.

He had an accident to arrange. That shouldn't be too difficult, not with an unsuspecting victim just waiting for him to choose the perfect moment. Perhaps even a fatality might be in order...never mind what Stanhope had prescribed.

Murder—perhaps that was the solution. It was no longer a game.

8

NATALIE HEARD THE DOOR slam shut behind her, just moments after she jumped off the steps onto the platform. Hitching her bag over her shoulder, she grabbed the handle of her suitcase and ran.

Hiding behind a conveniently wide pillar, Natalie watched the other passengers disembark, holding her breath against the possibility that Alex might have been looking. But no, her luck had finally turned. She'd made it! Only two women from the first-class section had left the train and one man from the car next to hers. He seemed vaguely familiar, but Natalie had seen a lot of people in the dining car and decided he was probably one of them. Either that, or he'd been in the line waiting for the bathroom that morning.

No one else got off, and the noisy engine was soon pulling away from the station, taking Alex with it.

So why did she feel so lousy?

Natalie shrugged aside the thought, determined to put Alex and last night's temptations behind her forever...or at least until her job was over. Then she'd have to see if he was still interested.

If he hadn't forgotten her.

That was one thing she'd never do—forget. It just wouldn't be possible, she was rapidly falling in love with the man.

But he was also the author of the puzzle, and quite possibly had entirely different motives for following her around. That was something else she couldn't afford to forget.

Stepping out from her hiding place, Natalie squared her shoulders and set off in search of a car rental facility. She probably could get by with taxis while in Edinburgh, but decided the trunk—or boot—would be a good place to keep her things until she had a better sense of where the puzzle was leading her.

Natalie had left the train at Haymarket, one stop short of the main Edinburgh station. The element of surprise would give her a head start, and she was determined to get at least three steps ahead of Alex and stay there!

She finally stumbled across the car rental agency and accepted the keys to a bright red sports car. She'd spent an hour poring over the city maps that Liz had sent along, and now pulled into the early-morning traffic with only the slightest of pauses. Driving on the left side was almost second nature by now, but it still gave her confidence to look into the mirror and find someone else following her lead. If she was wrong, she wasn't the only one!

With a minimum of trouble, Natalie found the city center and a parking lot convenient to the Royal Mile. First she needed breakfast. She studied her notes over her second cup of coffee. All in all, Edinburgh didn't look nearly as complicated as Oxford. Natalie even allowed herself to imagine finishing with Edinburgh the next day, hoping her fast work would keep her in front of Alex and out of his arms. Catching herself on the verge of yet another daydream, she grabbed a pencil and forced herself back to work.

The clue that had brought her to Edinburgh was the Scottish crown. Most people, to be sure, would immediately link it with the English crown on display at the Tower of London. They would be wrong, and Natalie was once again grateful she hadn't made that mistake.

She listed the remaining clues. First, and most unusual, was a castle. Not one of your typical, medieval castles that dotted the British landscape, but a storybook one. In fact, Natalie was positive it resembled one of the Bavarian King Ludwig's creations in Germany, and made a note to check out her theory. If she was correct, then the drawing probably represented castles in general and not a particular one in this area.

The other clues were an ax, a bolt from a door, a length of rope, a pearl earring, a candelabra with eleven candles and an ear. There was also a fanciful picture of an airplane looping the loop, and Natalie hoped that meant something easy like the city's airport. But the two items that interested her the most were a digital watch showing the time as two-thirty and a cap that reminded her of the style worn by the early Quakers in rural America.

As soon as a library opened she'd check out her hunch about the castle. Then she intended to locate the local headquarters or central meetinghouse of the Society of Friends. Checking the list that Liz had given her, Natalie saw she had half an hour before she could get into the public library, so she asked for another cup of coffee and once again reviewed her notes.

She didn't though, because niggling worries about where Alex was and when she'd run into him again claimed her thoughts.

IT WAS DINNERTIME before Natalie finally admitted defeat. Her hunch about the castle had been correct, but now she had to decide whether one or more clues combined to indicate a particular castle, or if the castle itself pointed toward other clues.

The Quaker idea was what had defeated her. While the Society of Friends had indeed originated in England—Leicestershire, to be precise—there was only a small following left in the Edinburgh area, and nothing Natalie unearthed about them seemed to be even remotely related to the other clues. A visit to their simple meetinghouse had been fruitless; it was scheduled for demolition next month. Alex could never have included a clue that would have ceased to exist before the book was published.

So, if not the Quakers, then what? Natalie no longer had the energy to speculate. And she still had to check in with Liz, find her hotel and something to eat.

Still, thanks to her early-morning maneuvering, there would be no Alex to worry about. Somehow Natalie wasn't excited by the prospect of a lonely evening in a strange city.

It only took a few minutes to drive from the Royal Mile to the hotel Liz had recommended, and Natalie was relieved to find it seasonally empty. Totally unlike the small, quaint accommodations in Oxford, this room was spacious, drafty and a little noisy. But the bathtub was enormous, the bed soft—and the telephone ringing.

Natalie eagerly reached a hand toward the jangling instrument, then feelings of hope and confusion made her hesitate for a long moment before answering.

If Alex had found her, then what?

And if he hadn't . . .

"You didn't tell me you were moving," the voice said, and Natalie had to wince at the well-deserved reprimand. Liz hated it when Natalie forgot to check in and never let her get away with it. "If you don't start calling in every day, I'll hire you another secretary."

Increasing the payroll seemed to be Liz's way of getting even, Natalie decided. "How did you find me?"

"The hotel in Oxford said you checked out, so I figured you'd eventually turn up in Edinburgh."

Liz was proving to be almost a better investigator than an office manager, Natalie realized.

"Oxford is finished."

"Congratulations. What's your timetable for Edinburgh?"

Natalie winced. Too bad she hadn't asked herself that question ten hours ago. "A couple of weeks, maybe more."

"That bad?" Liz, of course, didn't fall for the defeatist answer. But Natalie wasn't in the mood to be humored, and knew Liz wasn't very good at providing halftime pep talks. She also wasn't above hitting below the belt. "Want me to come take over?"

Natalie was tempted. "I'll have a bath first. If I don't drown, I'll give it another try."

"Stanhope said you were doing okay," Liz said encouragingly.

"Just okay?" Natalie was convinced that her work in Oxford had been nothing less than terrific.

"He's a conservative man."

"I'll bet." Thank goodness, she didn't have to call in with negative results. The last person she felt like talking with was Stanhope. She didn't even like talking about him so she changed the subject. "How's Mrs. Wilkins getting along?"

"Not bad. I couldn't find her watch the other day, so I'm giving it another shot this afternoon. But just in case, I went ahead and bought one of those cheap watches I was telling you about. It's purple with yellow dots."

"She'll love it." Natalie grinned, wishing she could be there to see Mrs. Wilkins's reaction.

"How's Alex?"

"Why do you ask?" Natalie stalled.

"Because I got the distinct impression that he was more than your average tour guide," her assistant replied smartly.

Natalie relented. Talking about him might ease the loneliness. She told Liz about the dinner in Oxford and about the train. Not everything, but just enough to convince the other woman that she was madly in love, but doing her best to avoid doing anything about it for the next three weeks.

Liz was appropriately delighted, and not at all sure Natalie was behaving properly.

"Are you sure you needed to ditch him?"

"I can't let him interfere."

"So who says he wants to?"

Natalie didn't answer. She couldn't.

NATALIE LINGERED at the north parapet, enjoying the view of the city and the river. It was a gorgeous day, and she found herself reluctant to join the rest of the tourists in their mad dash about the place.

What would Alex be doing today? Was he still in Edinburgh, or had he returned to Oxford? Natalie smiled to herself, torn between wanting to know and not daring to find out. Tilting her face to catch the full strength of the sun's early-morning rays, she daydreamed about meadows with wildflowers and babbling brooks and a picnic basket carried by a man she couldn't forget.

"You'd be surprised how easy it is to burn in this climate."

Her head snapped forward, then sideways, as Natalie homed in on the source of the comment. He was beside her, sharing the same few feet of stone wall, leaning contentedly against the ancient parapet as he stared at her from behind dark glasses.

"I thought I lost you," she murmured, not denying the pleasure she felt at his appearance.

Alex smiled. "Not for a minute." Grinning, he added, "Well, maybe a minute, but no longer."

"So where were you last night?"

"Perhaps it took a little more than a minute to catch up," he admitted sheepishly. "But I've got you now."

"And what do you plan on doing now that you've got me?" Natalie bit gently at her lower lip, then drew her tongue along its length. This game they were playing was exciting. The harder she ran, the harder he followed.

She wanted to stop running.

"There is always the satisfaction in a job well-done," he commented, taking off the dark glasses to let her feel his hot gaze. His eyes drifted down to her mouth as he remembered how her lips had tasted. The pink tip of her tongue moved slowly from one end of her mouth to the other before it disappeared inside. He watched intently.

That was where he wanted to be. Inside.

Natalie felt the draw of his hunger and knew it was real. She understood because it was no different from her own.

She stood there, not touching him. Just watching...waiting, oblivious to the city of Edinburgh at her feet.

"Could you take my picture?"

Natalie shook her head as if to clear it, dragging her gaze from Alex to focus it upon the woman standing beside her.

"Just one, with the cannon in the background," the stranger continued, thrusting the camera into her hands. "We don't have any cannons in Sioux City," she explained, then moved away to strike a pose in front of the ancient relic.

Natalie took the photograph. Returning the camera to its owner, she held a quick debate with herself. She could continue to work . . . or she could go with Alex. The invitation was there, the need was there. Every trace of indecision was gone.

As was Alex.

Whirling from the battlements to the nearby steps, her eyes searched the area. There wasn't a trace of him.

He had made the decision for her.

But Natalie now knew something else. *He would be back.*

THAT MORNING she had her first break after several exhausting hours in the library. The little white cap clearly pointed in one direction—Mary, Queen of Scots. Nearly all portraits of the tragic queen showed her wearing the cap with ribbons hanging down on either side. Added to that was the significance of the ax. Mary, Queen of Scots, had been beheaded in 1587.

Her third and last husband had been an earl—the Earl of Bothwell. This made sense because the ear added to the pearl earring in the puzzle could easily indicate the presence of the earl.

She had to keep researching castles. Checking her watch, Natalie decided to call Stanhope before it got much later. She wanted to catch him at his office. Somehow, calling him at his home gave their relationship an intimacy that made her vaguely uncomfortable.

"I figure the clues have something to do with castles," she said a little later to Stanhope trying to remain calm and professional. She would rather have laughed and shouted and jumped excitedly around the room, but Stanhope seemed to be playing this very cool, so she curbed her enthusiasm.

"Something," he agreed.

"It must be somewhere Mary and the earl met or stayed or whatever. I'll get back to the library and see what I can find."

"That's probably the best approach." Again, his total lack of enthusiasm made her wonder if she was headed in the right direction. But he wouldn't have agreed if she'd been wrong. That wasn't part of the deal. Maybe he would respond if she tried to be friendly.

"Have you ever been to Scotland?" There was a long pause, as if he hadn't heard her question. She repeated it.

"No."

Another long silence followed and Natalie decided that was as much as Stanhope was going to say. He wasn't exactly being unhelpful, she mused. Just acting as if her discovery didn't matter. His initial reaction to her call had been abrupt, too, almost as if she had interrupted something important.

But then, perhaps he did have more important things to think about. Just because the puzzle was the focus of her life, it didn't mean Stanhope was equally devoted.

"Call if you leave Edinburgh. Before you leave," was all Stanhope had to add.

Natalie agreed, wondering why he had felt it necessary to tell her that.

But she had more important things to worry about. In the first place, she had to *find* the clue that would make it possible to leave. Heaving her bag over her shoulder, Natalie left her room and headed back to the library.

The answer was there. She just had to find it . . . and recognize it when she did!

HE KNEW WHERE she was going now. Back to that bloody library! He hated that place. It was cold and damp and nearly impossible to hide in. But she was going, and there wasn't a thing he could do to stop her.

Not unless he hot-wired a nearby car and ran her down. Or shoved her off the curb into the speeding traffic.

Or just pushed his knife between her ribs.

But he might get caught doing any of those things in broad daylight, and the last one wouldn't look even remotely like an accident. That was important, because then the police would be looking for a murderer. Besides, Stanhope had told him to scare her, not kill her.

Well, he'd make his own decision about that. For now he continued to follow her, watching as she entered the library. But this time he didn't go in. He couldn't.

He had to arrange an accident. It was time she realized she wasn't alone.

116   *Two Can Play*

SHE CALLED LIZ, ignoring the childish impulse to gloat over her victory in a call to Stanhope. He could wait, and she *knew* she was right.

"I'm going to a place called Borthwick Castle. This afternoon. It's the last place the earl and Mary were together, before he went nuts and she lost her head altogether. Anyway, now it's a fancy hotel."

"Mary who?"

"Queen of Scots, of course. Who did you think I was talking about?"

"Heaven knows," came the reply, but Natalie was so excited that she ignored the sarcasm.

"Anyway, it was built in 1430—2:30, if you don't use the twenty-four-hour clock. So I'm heading there now." This time Liz asked for clarification, and Natalie patiently explained how the sketch of the watch that read 2:30 was connected to a castle built in 1430; 14:30 was 2:30 on a conventional watch.

"Was Stanhope as excited as you are?"

"Er, not quite," she mumbled, then explained she'd decided not to make the call until later.

"Isn't this the same man who is supposed to be helping you? What if you're wrong?"

"I'm *not* wrong!"

"Then why don't you call him?" Liz made it sound like the only sensible thing to do. Especially because Borthwick Castle was several miles outside Edinburgh, and the trip would be a huge waste of time if it proved to be a false trail.

"I will. Later. After I get a better idea of what I'm looking for there." And then, because Liz clearly didn't understand, she explained. "He has a tendency to dampen my enthusiasm."

"You mean he doesn't jump up and down when you get it right?" Liz asked, accustomed to Natalie's natural exuberance when whatever she was working on happened to be going well.

"Something like that."

"Would it help if I jumped up and down?" she offered.

"Probably not. You never do. It would be out of character. Besides, that would be too much like exercise."

"There's that," Liz agreed.

"Speaking of exercise, I'm going to head out there now, so I have time for a run before dinner."

"Sounds nice."

Natalie giggled. The word *run* wasn't even in Liz's vocabulary, never mind *nice run*.

She hung up the phone before Liz had a chance to ask about Alex.

9

NATALIE PUMPED the brake pedal again, but nothing happened.

Or rather, the car picked up more speed on the downhill slope and then screeched around the curve at the bottom. Natalie hung on to the wheel with both hands until the road straightened, then reached down to pull on the emergency brake.

Still nothing.

The brakes were gone. Both of them. Or all of them, she really didn't know enough about cars in general to say which. Nor did she have the time to care. Not now, when the car was screaming out of control along this quiet country lane, just a few miles south of Edinburgh.

Screaming out of control was something of an exaggeration. At the moment she wasn't even over the speed limit. But as far as Natalie was concerned, even though the road was deserted and the hills were no more than gentle mounds, having no brakes was dangerous.

And since she didn't know what was around the next corner and couldn't count on having the road to herself indefinitely, Natalie was a little concerned.

Alex would know what to do, she thought, then remembered the hair-raising ride in the Land-Rover. Well, perhaps not.

Natalie figured she could either drive her way out of this or drive into something.

Preferably a haystack. She didn't see one, certainly not in the middle of the road.

But that didn't mean there wouldn't be one around the next curve. Hope springs eternal, or something like that. Natalie was amazed by the spurious notions that crossed her mind. It was probably like having your life flash before your eyes, she mused, only slightly disturbed by their triteness.

Steering through a series of tight turns, she tried to use the road to slow her down, but every time she made some headway, there would be another of those gentle hills and she'd pick up all the speed she'd just managed to lose. Natalie considered turning off the motor, but wasn't sure whether doing that would lock the wheels or just strip the transmission. She'd definitely lose the power steering, and that idea didn't appeal to her at all.

Of course, this was no time to berate herself for renting an automatic drive. Critiques would come later...if there *was* a later.

The end came suddenly.

Natalie found the only big hill in the neighborhood.

The car coasted to a near stop about two-thirds of the way up and she drove it onto the shoulder, until the wheels sank firmly into deep mud.

Now it was no longer her problem—just the rental company's. Lucky for them she was on a mission. Otherwise she might have taken the time to make them pay for their shoddy maintenance.

It wasn't as if she was hurt. She wasn't even particularly scared, she told herself, proud to notice the trembling had finally ceased. At least she hadn't been in the city, where traffic and pedestrians would have forced her to plow into something solid—probably something that would have hurt a lot. But Natalie had chosen a quiet road because she was tired of the noise and hustle of the city, and for the better part of the drive had enjoyed the view.

She still liked the view. But the angle was different now that she was on foot and the sun was setting.

Her real problem was getting herself—and her belongings—the rest of the way to Borthwick Castle. From there she could arrange to rent another car if she needed it. One with a gearshift and clutch.

Pulling the map out of the car, Natalie spread it on the hood and checked her position. It wasn't as bad as she'd thought. Borthwick Castle was a couple of miles to the east. But she could only count on another thirty minutes or so of daylight, so she stuffed the map back into the car and went around to open the boot.

Boot. That brought a grin. Amazing how quickly one's vocabulary could adapt! Dragging her suitcase around so she could open it, Natalie pulled out her running clothes and shoes, then hid behind the car to change so that no one could surprise her.

"AND YOUR LUGGAGE, Miss Tracy?"

"It's in the boot," she replied calmly. Then she explained where the boot was.

Hot, sweaty and very, very thirsty, Natalie leaned against the Formica-topped reception desk and waited for someone to drive her back to the car. After first hearing where it was parked, they had offered to drive there without her and collect her belongings, but Natalie wasn't absolutely sure she could describe the exact location and it was getting too dark for guessing games.

With the typical British respect for privacy, no one had asked why her car was parked on a hill in the middle of nowhere, and Natalie hadn't offered an explanation. For that matter, she'd also omitted the part about the ditch. She was saving the minor details for the people at the rental company. They deserved to be the first to hear exactly what she thought of them.

The trip to the car was accomplished efficiently, and Natalie was soon back at the reception desk. "We've given you the Mary, Queen of Scots Room." The clerk beamed at Natalie.

Clearly this was supposed to be an honor. Natalie wasn't sure she agreed, particularly as the unfortunate queen had spent some of her last days of freedom in that room. But she was attracted by the possibility that the room might help with the puzzle.

"Dinner is seven-thirty for eight."

Natalie had been in Britain long enough to realize that meant drinks at seven-thirty, dinner at eight. More or less. Checking her watch, she discovered she had exactly thirty minutes to wash away all the grime. The thought didn't appeal to her, but she was resigned. And hungry.

"Is Mr. Garrick dining at the castle tonight?" she asked. Alex had obviously had a hand in the arrangements.

The clerk checked her list, then nodded. "Yes. He's signed in for dinner."

Natalie thanked her, then turned to follow the man carrying her luggage. Sometime between leaving Edinburgh and arriving here she'd realized Alex would be waiting for her.

The porter led her directly to the Great Hall. Natalie tried not to gawk at its sheer magnificence, but failed miserably. Passing the long table, already set for dinner, she gazed with astonishment at the fireplace at the far end. She'd read about it in a book on Borthwick, but hadn't been able to picture it. Flanked by sofas and low tables, the deep-set structure was easily twenty feet high. Glancing up at the chandeliers as she went, Natalie forced herself onward.

Climbing the ancient tower stairs to her room, Natalie was grateful that all she had to do was lift one foot after the other. Suitcases would have been beyond her, and she was amazed that the man in front of her managed to make the ascent without getting stuck or dropping something.

Finally they reached her room, and she saw how queens had lived centuries ago. Or at the very least, saw how Mary, Queen of Scots must have lived. Thanking the man for his help, Natalie took a minute to explore her fascinating quarters. The huge, canopied bed first caught her attention, but the closet that covered a whole wall was equally enchanting. The window recesses were furnished with wooden benches and raised slightly above the level of the main room. Natalie walked the length of one, delighted by the triptych-style mirror set under one window. But a look into the mirror persuaded Natalie that she had a lot to do just to make herself presentable for dinner, so she turned away and got busy.

The knock at her door came just as she was winding down her lecture to the rental car company. Natalie shouted, "Come in," and continued her diatribe. Seated on the bed with the telephone receiver resting on one shoulder, she watched Alex enter.

When she didn't scream, jump up in surprise or do whatever else he might have expected, he leaned against the wall and listened.

"You can send someone to the reception desk. No, I'm not going to take you out there myself. I'm too busy.

They're too busy, too. But I marked a map and left it with them."

Glancing up at Alex, she smiled to tell him she'd missed him and pointed at the drinks tray, in case he wanted to help himself. He didn't, but Natalie couldn't help but see him count the empty Coke and ginger ale bottles she'd left on top of the refrigerator—the results of her recent exercise. She stifled a chuckle at the question in his eyes, then returned her attention to the telephone.

"And don't forget to bring a tow truck. You'll need it. No, thank you. If I need another car, I'll get one elsewhere." Receiving the impression that the rather excited man at the other end of the line would talk all night if she let him, Natalie said thank-you and hung up the phone.

"Problems?" he asked.

"Nothing important." She slid off the bed and opened the closet to find her shoes, remembering too late that she hadn't taken the time to unpack. Though she tried to conceal it, Alex unnerved her to the point where simple things seemed to elude her. Like shoes.

In fact, the record-breaking shower and shampoo had left her with just minutes to blow-dry her hair and add a touch of lipstick and mascara. Had he arrived three minutes earlier, Alex might have caught her pulling on her slip and dress. Natalie knew she looked terrific in the simple, forest-green silk, and somehow that was very important tonight.

So why didn't he tell her as much?

Privately acknowledging that she'd look even better with shoes, she padded across the room and into one of the recessed alcoves, where the porter had left her suitcase. Naturally her shoes were at the bottom, so she began to dig.

Slipping into the high-heeled pumps, she dismissed the idea that flat shoes might be more sensible on those tower steps. But stealing a glance at Alex, she wondered whether it mattered, after all. He was watching her, his face devoid of expression, his body casually relaxed against the wall, as if he hadn't a serious thought in his head.

Dressed and shod, Natalie ignored his silence and decided she could live without compliments. "Are you here to make sure I don't fall down the steps and break my neck?"

"Partly," he admitted, letting her know with a glance that her heels were both aesthetically appreciated and practically discredited. "You might try walking barefoot to the ground floor."

"Makes sense," she agreed, only too happy to take his suggestion. "Why else did you stop by?"

"You don't know?" he asked softly, shifting sideways until he could reach the open door and begin to push it shut.

She'd been wrong. Again. What Natalie had read as lack of interest was tightly controlled need. She could see that now.

She reveled in it. She wanted him. She loved him.

Startled, Natalie grinned at his daring and challenged him in turn. "If you close that door now, you'll never know if I fainted from hunger or ecstasy."

"I would," he murmured huskily.

"But I'd still be hungry," she answered, reasonably sure she wouldn't care, either.

He eyed Natalie, then the door, clearly weighing the pros and cons.

"Dinner won't last forever," Alex finally said, pushing the door open with obvious reluctance.

"I know," she replied softly, bending to remove her shoes before he could see the inevitable blush high on her cheeks.

DINNER WAS AN EXPERIENCE Natalie wouldn't have missed for anything. Well, almost anything.

When they finally reached the ground floor, Natalie guessed the cocktail hour was nearly over. And that was a shame, she thought, because she'd ignored the alcoholic beverages in her room in favor of refreshing sodas, and was now ready and willing to bolster her courage with a glass or two of whatever was going. But she needn't have worried. By the time she replaced her shoes and allowed Alex to escort her in to join the small crowd gathered around the fireplace, a second round of drinks was being announced.

Dinner, apparently, was delayed. That was probably a tactical move on the part of the management, gently encouraging otherwise reticent guests to join in the merriment by means of an extended cocktail hour. Whatever the reason, it worked. By the time they moved to the table, Natalie felt much better than she had several hours ago.

Alex never left her side. That was enough to keep her glowing *without* the aid of a second cocktail.

While the hotel was not quite full, there were still twelve guests for dinner, and Natalie was tired enough to find learning all the names a bit of a chore. It was worth the effort though, especially when she heard all about the castle from a couple who had already spent several nights there. And after dinner there would be a tour of the premises.

Tomorrow was soon enough to get serious about work. Tonight she was definitely off duty.

The long table Natalie had seen earlier stood in the center of the Great Hall. She found herself seated beside Alex about halfway down, and did her best to pay attention to the American businessman on her right.

But it was difficult, because every time they got involved in a discussion of where they were from and what they were doing in Europe, Natalie found herself distracted by a light touch on her wrist or elbow, a reminder that Alex was there, watching and waiting. Not that he showed with even a glance that he was the slightest bit aware of her presence. From what Natalie could see, the elderly schoolteacher from Dover was delighted to have Alex's rapt attention during the sumptuous meal.

While Alex might have been pretending to ignore her, her wineglass was never empty. When she covered the silver goblet with her hand to protest, he asked, "Are you driving?"

That made a funny kind of sense, so she let him pour. "I realize, of course, that you're trying to get me drunk."

"I wouldn't dream of it," he protested, smiling at the raised eyebrows that clearly signaled her disbelief. "I just think you need to relax a little."

"Sure I do." Any more relaxed and she'd be sliding off her chair.

"Besides," he whispered seductively, "bedtime is hours away. We've still got the tour of the house and coffee to endure. You'll be sober when you need to be," he promised.

"The tour," she echoed. "I'd forgotten."

"You'll like it," he assured her.

Natalie grabbed her wine and took an enormous gulp. Like it? He was a master of understatement.

"The tour of the house, Natalie," he repeated smoothly. "Particularly the ghost story. That's the best part."

"Ghost story?" she asked nervously, silently rebuking herself for letting him rattle her and get away with it. The not-so-subtle reference to their earlier conversation in her bedroom had had her jumping to conclusions. As he'd intended, she realized.

Of course there was a ghost story. Mary, Queen of Scots, probably haunted everyone who slept in her bed. Or in her room, Natalie amended. The bed was not four hundred years old. At least, she hoped it wasn't.

The bed again. Natalie winced, uncomfortably aware of the persistence with which that subject came up.

"I wouldn't dream of spoiling it for you." He flicked a stray curl off her shoulder before turning to speak to the schoolteacher.

A slightly bemused Natalie followed Alex on the castle tour, pleased to learn the ghost story was not about Mary, Queen of Scots, but that beastly earl she'd married. Not to mention the servant girl he'd managed to put into the family way and the ghastly thing he'd done to hide his misdeed from the queen and everyone else.

The story continued with a twentieth-century follow-up that involved a Norwegian girl—staying in the same room where the earl had murdered the servant—who'd had a terrible nightmare and woken up, covered in blood. The white-jacketed waiter conducting the tour finished the tale in a hushed voice. "And to this day she is still in a mental hospital."

By the end of the tour Natalie was sober—and thankful to be spending the night in Mary, Queen of Scots's room.

Standing alone on the balcony that overlooked the Great Hall, Natalie shivered at the ghostly images conjured up by her overactive imagination. It was here that Mary and her husband had spent their last days together, and from here she'd escaped disguised as a page boy. But the freedom that followed had been short; she'd spent a score of years as Queen Elizabeth's prisoner.

Natalie wondered which had been worse, the twenty, long years of imprisonment or the final, few moments before the ax fell. Shuddering, she tried to put the events back into their proper, historical perspective, wishing she had stayed with the guided tour. But she'd needed a few moments alone and had wanted to view the candle-lit hall just once more. In the light of day, the entire atmosphere of the castle would change.

For now she wanted to savor the spirit of passion and defiance she felt in the aftermath of the stories she'd just heard. Mary and her earl had danced together, they'd been told, in the reception room that connected Mary's bedroom with that of her husband.

Natalie wondered if Alex was staying there.

"I told you you'd be sober," he breathed into her ear.

Natalie jumped the requisite mile, then slowly turned to face him. "I really wish you'd quit doing that."

"Doing what?" he asked innocently.

"Sneaking up behind me and scaring me half to death."

"Now when have I done that?"

"On the hill near your home," she began, all of a sudden recalling how she had wanted him that night.

Dragging the tip of her tongue along suddenly dry lips, she tried to remember what she'd been saying. The fiercely hungry eyes that were trained on her mouth took away her breath, stole her resistance and made her want only one thing.

One man.

Alex didn't touch her. He didn't dare. Dragging his gaze away from the tantalizing invitation of her mouth, he lowered his eyelids and shut out her silent question. Knowing that she already knew just how badly he wanted her, he wanted her to take the first steps now. Knowing his own mind, he wanted to be sure she knew hers.

Looking at her now, he thought he had his answer. Her eyes were sparkling with an eagerness that he couldn't miss . . . and couldn't resist.

"We can skip coffee," he suggested. Another ten minutes without touching Natalie—perhaps not even that long—was about all he could endure.

"I think there's brandy in the bar in my room."

"Are you sure?"

Natalie knew what he was asking. "Not really," she said with a smile that trembled over her lips. "But if not, I know I saw a bottle of champagne."

"That will do." He held out his hand, waiting for the final gesture of trust.

"In a pinch," she agreed, smiling more easily as she placed her hand in his.

"YOU JUST WANT the ghosts to get me first," he kidded when she stood aside to let him enter the room.

"There's that," she admitted. "You might look under the bed to make sure they're not hiding, and you can check that monster closet, too. There's enough room in there for ten ghosts!"

"Frightened of the dark, Natalie?"

"Of course not," she said quickly, tossing the shoes she carried into a corner as Alex closed the door. "But I probably won't sleep until I know, one way or the other. And I'm not above bribing you to do the looking for me!"

"What happens if I find one?" he asked curiously.

"You get to keep it."

"What's the bribe?"

She didn't answer.

Alex strolled over to the wardrobe, firmly grasped the barley-twist handles and dramatically flung the doors wide open. "See," he said. "No ghosts."

"You haven't looked under the bed," She handed him a small snifter of brandy.

"You're right." Taking a sip from the glass in his hand, Alex moved toward the bed, grasping her hand to draw her along with him. Pushing her down to sit on the mattress, he relieved her of the brandy she held and set both of their drinks on a nearby table.

"Wait there," he said, then dropped to the floor, so that his eyes were level with her feet.

There was a long silence.

"What are you doing?" she asked nervously, when he didn't move.

"Deciding."

"Deciding what?" she asked. Deciding whether or not to tell her about the ghosts under the bed?

"Deciding whether I should kiss your toes."

"My what?"

Something wet and warm trailed across the tops of her toes, then back again.

It should have been silly. Or absurd.

It wasn't.

Instead it was terribly, wonderfully erotic. And exciting.

His mouth slid wetly upwards, following warm, strong fingers past her calves until they reached her knees. They received the same, loving attention as had her toes, pitching Natalie in to a contrary state of relaxed arousal. The fine weave of her hose enhanced the unreal experience of his openmouthed caress, and she shivered at the sensation.

When he slipped a hand under the hem of her skirt, she fell back onto her elbows, only half-conscious of her pleading murmur.

"Is it easier now?" he asked softly, the husky timbre of his voice lulling her into complete surrender.

"Easier?" Startled by the nearness of his voice, she opened her eyes to find him bent over her. One knee crushed the mattress at her hip, while his other leg was firmly anchored on the other side of her knees, capturing her with his strength, holding her with his skill. His hand still rested warmly just above her knee.

"Yes. Easier to imagine us together. Making love," he continued patiently. "I thought you were a little tense earlier."

"Oh." Fixing her gaze on the second button of his shirt, Natalie marveled how he had conquered her nervousness. A little kiss, when she was least expecting it . . . where she was least expecting it.

But she wanted him now, and wanted him to know it. Reaching up with trembling fingers to grasp his silk tie, Natalie firmly pulled his mouth down to meet hers.

At first he was surprised, then entranced, taking her lips with barely restrained hunger. He had to be careful, he reminded himself. If he let go, he'd be inside her in just moments, pushing and stroking them to the peak before they'd had a chance to enjoy the climb.

And he wanted to enjoy her. All of her. Plunging his tongue into her hot, wet mouth, he promised her of the excitement to come.

Natalie was still in a vulnerable half-reclining position, leaning heavily against the arm Alex was using to keep her from falling back. The steady rhythm of his thrusting tongue nearly drove her mad, but she responded in kind, challenging him to continue. Her fingers crept around his neck to tangle in the short curls at his nape, then slipped inside the collar of his shirt.

That wasn't enough. It wasn't even close. Dragging her lips away from the overwhelming assault of his mouth, she tried to pull back—just far enough to see the knot of his tie. But even as her fingers began to tackle the problem, his lips found new targets, diverting her attention, making it impossible to concentrate. Wet, warm kisses were trailed over her eyes, and she had to rely entirely on her sense of touch.

"Leave it!" he growled, but she kept up her efforts to loosen the silken knot. She wanted to touch him, needed to know his body would respond. Almost desperate, she pulled at the buttons underneath the tie. Finally she succeeded. Two, then three buttons were freed, and she slipped her hand into the gap, delighting in the soft curls she found covering his chest.

This was Alex, the man she loved. Feeling his thundering heartbeat under her fingers, Natalie rejoiced.

This was the fire and passion of a man who desired her, totally.

Loving him as she did, Natalie dreamed of turning his passion into love for her. Finding the hard nub of an erect, male nipple under her fingers, she stroked it lightly.

"Damn it, woman! Don't do that!" He dragged her hand away from his chest, then stared at the offending fingers as if wondering how they'd gotten into his hand. "I can't *think* when you do that!"

"You're not supposed to be thinking." Natalie was breathing hard, conscious of the hand that had returned to her knee.

Against her mouth, between hard, fast kisses, he tried to explain. "If I don't think, if I just let go . . ."

Natalie moved her hand again, back to that lovely nest of curls on his chest. "So let go," she murmured.

He tugged her hand away once more, whispering threats of what he'd do. "Touch me again and I won't be able to stop. I'll just throw your skirt up and pull down my zip and plunge into you. I need you so much, I won't be able to stop."

But it wasn't a threat. It was a promise. So Natalie smiled, daring him to let go. The thought of being that close, of having Alex inside her . . .

Determined to break his control, Natalie offered her lips to his hungry mouth, dragging her nails across his shoulders and down his back.

He discovered the silken gap between her stockings and the lace edge of her panties and was driving her insane, lightly drawing his knuckles and the tips of his fingers over this exposed skin. Falling back against the strength of his supporting arm, Natalie breathed unevenly, blindly seeking his mouth with her lips yet again.

"This is how I want it," he whispered, drawing circles on her silken thigh, pausing to pull up her skirt so he could see what he was doing. "I want you hot and mindless. I want you to feel what I'm feeling, to burn like I'm burning." Again he thrust his tongue into her mouth, whispering promises of the heights they would reach together.

The words sank slowly through the sensual web of desire he was creating. Natalie barely heard them. Sliding her tongue along the bottom of his, she grasped his shoulders with fingers that were trembling. This need inside her overwhelmed all thought, left her totally open to his desire.

But she trusted him, and was rewarded with wave after wave of sensual pleasure.

"Open your legs for me, love. I want to touch you."

The shock of his request struck something wildly primitive deep inside her, and she obeyed. Natalie gasped when he slid first one finger, then another under the edge of her lacy panties, writhing with uncontrolled pleasure when his tongue returned to explore her mouth.

When his knowing fingers moved through the damp curls and found the nub of her pleasure she was unable to suppress her moan of ecstasy. He swallowed the low sound of excitement, but then his mouth left hers and she whimpered.

"Hush, love," he soothed, then proceeded to excite her even more. Finding the hard tip of her breast that thrust against the fabric of her dress, he took it between his teeth. Natalie cried out again. As his lips began to suck gently at the erect nipple, his fingers slid deep inside her.

Natalie gasped helplessly, arching her hips to the rhythm of his hand. He sent her to the peak, leaving her trembling for just moments before he began again, driving her up and over the top in a matter of seconds.

She was soaring, shivering, holding Alex so closely she never wanted to let him go.

When he levered himself away from her, she wanted to cry out. From the edge of the bed she watched him tear off his clothes and marveled at the strength and sheer beauty of his body. He needed her. Standing naked before her, he couldn't hide it.

Alex stood there for a long moment, watching her. She felt his eyes slide lazily over her disheveled clothing, saw them blaze with fiery possession when they glimpsed the damp circles surrounding her nipples, the creamy thighs highlighted by her satin garters. His passionate gaze stung her into yet another level of awareness, but this time she needed to do more than take.

She needed to give.

Reaching out a hand, she pleaded. And finally he came to her.

In seconds Alex had removed her clothes and pulled back the covers to lay her gently upon the sheets. "I want you so much," he said huskily, sliding down beside her.

Holding Natalie still beside him, Alex shut his eyes and counted to ten. And again. It didn't work, but then, he really hadn't expected it to. Having her this close, the length of her body molded against his own, he simply couldn't wait any longer. He rolled until Natalie was beneath him and with his knee urged her to part her legs.

He slipped his hands under her, grasping the firm curves of her bottom, and lifted her to meet him. Hearing her gasp, he opened his eyes to Natalie's emerald gaze. With a single thrust, he entered her.

She was wet and warm and welcoming, and so tight he thought he'd die.

Natalie held her breath, absolutely convinced that nothing in her life would ever be the same again. This felt so good, so right. Lying here with Alex, a part of him now, just as he was a part of her.

And when he finally began to move, she arched up to him, joining in the rhythm that drove them closer than any two humans could possibly be. He took her mouth, she gave it willingly. Wildly, excitedly, they climbed steadily higher until finally they shattered ordinary boundaries.

ALEX STRUGGLED against the temptation to stay right where he was, but decided crushing Natalie into the mattress wouldn't serve any good purpose. Regretfully he pulled himself away, smiling gently as he saw she was already asleep. Her breathing was even, and he thought he even detected a slight snore. Careful not to disturb her any more than necessary, he turned her sideways and pulled her, spoon fashion, into the warmth of his body.

The lights were still on, but they weren't too bright, and Alex didn't think Natalie cared one way or the other. Besides, to turn them out he'd have to get out of bed and leave her.

That was out of the question.

Alex didn't think he'd leave Natalie ever again. The reason behind all of his earlier caution was finally clear. The gentle courting he'd planned, the effort he'd taken to ensure Natalie came to him freely and willingly. Now everything made sense.

Natalie was more than just a woman who strongly attracted him. She was more than a challenge—a great deal more.

She was the woman he loved. She was the woman he wanted to marry.

Alex didn't know how it had happened. He really didn't even care. Knowing would change nothing, although the simple fact of loving her accounted for the somewhat adolescent game of follow my leader they'd been playing since they met.

What was really important was discovering if she felt the same. If she didn't, then he would make her love him.

Alex was planning his campaign when the telephone rang, startling Natalie out of a deep sleep, out of his arms.

10

"YOU didn't call."

Natalie had grabbed the telephone before it could ring twice, shaken by the brutal invasion of her fantasy.

But it hadn't been a fantasy. It had been real.

Alex was still there, in her bed, proof that her imagination hadn't run amok. She felt the intensity of his gaze as she sat with her back to him. Natalie couldn't resist glancing over her shoulder, and was rewarded by a hot, exciting flare of passion in his eyes. Raised on one elbow with the covers draped low on his hips, his body was poised for her return.

Alex presented a convincing argument for hanging up on Stanhope.

Tiny shivers of anticipation raced up and down her spine, but Natalie forced herself to turn away before the intolerable noise in her ear rose yet another decibel. Alex wasn't going anywhere, and the sooner she got rid of Stanhope, the sooner she could return to the warm welcome of his arms.

"You didn't call like you promised!" the voice in her ear insisted. Natalie reluctantly dragged her thoughts away from Alex. Grabbing her robe from the foot of the bed, she pulled it around her shoulders before she froze.

Something was definitely odd about the man's behavior. First there had been his unnecessary reminder

to call from Edinburgh—a cue she'd ignored more out
of stubbornness than for any concrete reason.

And now this. His words held a whining overtone.
She didn't like it, and not just because it was undigni-
fied for a grown man.

Something was wrong.

"How did you know I'd be here?" she countered.

"Your secretary. At least you managed to keep her
informed," he huffed, not troubling to disguise his irritation. "You must keep me informed about your
whereabouts."

Natalie didn't bother to tell him her whereabouts
were her own business, and should concern Stanhope
only in the context of the puzzle. She stifled the impulse to remind Stanhope that his job was to give guidance and direction. What it didn't include was calling
her in the middle of the night to hand out unsolicited
criticism and accusations.

"I'll call you in the morning when I'm awake," she
said, holding on to her temper by a thread.

But he clearly wasn't ready to be put off. "Report
now."

"Listen, Mr. Stanhope. I said I'd call you in the
morning. The more I think about it, the better that
sounds. I'll call you first thing, British time," she added
for emphasis, realizing that would make it before dawn
in New York. "Then perhaps you can try to think
straight when you pick up the phone in the middle of
your sleep."

Slamming down the receiver, Natalie took a deep
breath, willing her irritation to disappear. It took three
tries before she was satisfied with the result, but the
delay was worthwhile; as she shrugged the robe from

her shoulders and turned back to Alex, Natalie was smiling.

"You're cheating." Was-that a faint tremor in his voice? she wondered. But it was the look in his eyes that really captured her attention. They were flat and hard.

"What?" The accusation hung heavily in the air between them, echoing unmercifully in her thoughts. *What was he talking about?* Natalie was stunned, almost speechless.

"I said you're cheating," he repeated harshly as he threw back the covers and vaulted out of bed. "As in defrauding, swindling, conning. Or, as you Americans might say, screwing. You're screwing the people who engaged you. You and Stanhope." Jerking on his pants and shirt, he fastened them hurriedly.

Suddenly the pieces fell together, and the small part of her mind that wasn't frozen in disbelief understood. She had to make him understand. "The contact between Stanhope and me was designed by his boss. We're doing nothing wrong."

At first he didn't appear to have heard. Finding his socks near the chair, he rammed them into a pocket, then stared again at Natalie. The diamond-hard glint in his eyes told her in no uncertain terms that he didn't believe her. "That's a lie," he said flatly. "Another one. They wouldn't have gone to all the trouble of a test and then supplied you with the answers."

"He's not giving me answers," she replied softly.

But he ignored her. He obviously didn't want to hear. He had found her guilty without letting her explain the truth.

Natalie fell silent. If Alex could so easily believe she would do something so utterly contemptible, there wasn't any point in arguing. By believing the worst, he was showing her precisely how little respect he'd had for her in the first place. Her dreams . . . her hopes that he might somehow love her in return . . . everything was ruined.

After that it somehow didn't matter what he thought. The part of her that wasn't totally frozen took charge, compelling her to maintain her silence as the barrage continued, drawing her attention to little things like the robe that was open to her waist. Trembling fingers plucked at the edges, pulling it steadily up her arms until she was covered again. Natalie kept her silence, praying he would leave before the hurt got out of control.

"You had me fooled. Completely." Stuffing the silk tie into his jacket pocket, he shuffled around until he located his shoes. Shoving his feet into the polished loafers, he caught and held her gaze once more. His eyes were still hard, cold and accusing, daring her to contradict him.

"What's wrong? Didn't they give Stanhope all the answers? Did he think I'd whisper the answers in my sleep?" He spoke without a hint of emotion now, lashing out mercilessly until she was holding herself together by willpower alone. "I was right from the start. You needed me, and not just to warm your bed."

The real pain came from knowing that Alex hadn't stopped for one second to consider he might be wrong, hadn't believed her, even when she'd told him the truth. He simply knew he was right, because he had expected this from the beginning. Natalie remembered the first time he had accused her of trying to get close to him. Now she realized he had never dismissed the idea.

Finally Natalie understood what had been bothering her about Alex from the beginning.

He had followed her because he wanted to prove he was right. Nothing more, nothing less. Now that he'd accomplished that, he was leaving.

His fingers resting on the doorknob, Alex paused. "I haven't quite figured out what Stanhope gets out of this." Shooting her another calculating glance, he asked, "Are you splitting the fee? Or is it the treasure he's after?"

Dark eyes narrowed and impaled her with a final thrust. "Did you think I'd just stand aside and let you waltz off with it? Is that what you and Stanhope planned, that I'd lead you to it, if you let me sleep with you?"

Laughing bitterly, he turned the handle and pulled the door open. "You took a stupid chance, Natalie. Take it from someone who writes about calculated opportunities. *You* should have come to *my* room. Then I might have never figured it out."

Flicking his eyes to the tumble of sheets and blankets and back to her pale face, he asked softly, "Was it worth it, Natalie?"

He didn't wait for an answer. But then, of course, he didn't expect one.

He already had it.

FINDING THE LIGHT SWITCHES had been the hardest part.

And while the rest wasn't exactly a snap, she could at least say she had done it. At first, when she had descended the spiral staircase and pushed open the door into the Great Hall, there had been only a faint glow from the waning fire to light her way. Long shadows filled the corners and alcoves of the enormous room, making her search for the control panel almost painfully frightening.

But with the lights finally on, calm determination took over and she concentrated on the matter at hand. Natalie was here to solve a puzzle, and she intended to do so before morning.

That was the only way she could legitimately leave Borthwick Castle.

The sooner she finished *The Quest*, the sooner she could return to Boston...escape from Alex and the lies he believed. His absolute certainty that she was guilty of cheating had shattered her. Now she funneled her remaining energy into completing the treasure hunt.

She could do it. She had never meant to let Alex interfere. Now, before it was too late, she had to put him out of her thoughts . . . out of her life.

Starting at the top of the list, Natalie examined each word as if it were the most important combination of characters in the world. Concentration. That was the key. Thinking about Alex was counterproductive. Work was healing, success was restorative. Love was unimportant.

Love was pain.

FOUR HOURS and thirty-seven minutes later, Natalie thought she had the answer.

If she was right, she also had a way to translate the Oxford clue of The Pleiades.

The answer for Edinburgh was eleven. Pictured in the massive painting that decorated the better part of one wall of the Great Hall was a candelabra with eleven candles. And Mary, Queen of Scots had escaped from Borthwick on 11 June 1567.

Getting that far hadn't been easy, but now, reviewing her reasoning for the tenth time, she knew there was no other choice. Deleting the clues of the castle, ax,

pearl earring, hat, ear and watch, she had been left with
a bolt, the rope and a candelabra, not to mention the
airplane looping the loop.

The bolt had puzzled her the most, until she had realized it could be a verb. Mary had escaped by lowering herself from a window, dressed in the clothes of a
page—she had bolted from the threatening lords.

In the end she was left with the two clues containing
the #11 and the airplane. So if *eleven* was the answer
for Edinburgh, then the solution for Oxford was
seven—from The Pleiades or Seven Sisters.

The airplane looping a loop seemed to be related to
nothing. Just like the round table from the Oxford section.

Returning to her room, Natalie dialed Stanhope's
home number. She knew she'd drag him from a warm
bed, but there was no satisfaction in that. All that mattered was confirming her guesses and leaving the castle
before breakfast—before Alex called New York and
discovered for himself the true nature of her associa-
tion with the publisher.

She was right to discard the airplane as a red herring; she had solved the part of the puzzle that re-
quired her presence in Edinburgh. For a man who had
been so abrasive just hours before, Stanhope was all
sweetness and light, congratulating Natalie on her
amazing progress and encouraging her to set out for the
Lake District at first light.

It was as if last night had never happened. Carefully
replacing the receiver, Natalie agreed that was a good
strategy.

Pretending last night had never happened might be
the key to her survival.

EARLY IN THE AFTERNOON, Natalie pulled into the parking lot of the Grasmere's Tourist Information Centre. She was tired and hungry, impatient to get on with the puzzle.

She was no longer playing a game. The challenge to solve each clue no longer excited her; success only brought her grim satisfaction. With over two weeks remaining, she was gaining both in confidence and experience—experience that had taught her first to study the clues in relation to the published guides and references, then concentrate on one or two.

Natalie rapidly accomplished her mission at the modern facility, and was settled in her hotel room in record time. Opening the window to let in some fresh, spring air, she was only vaguely aware of the beauty of the garden below her. She had no energy to recall Wordsworth's "golden daffodils," signature of an English spring.

It had been a long morning, although the drive from Edinburgh was not difficult. The hard part had been getting away from the castle before Alex came down for breakfast, but with the cooperation of the night porter, she had located another rental car and was on the road well before eight o'clock.

The effects of a sleepless night and the lack of food were beginning to show, she knew. Her hands shook slightly and her head was spinning. Opting for a bath to calm the shakes, Natalie steadfastly ignored her rumbling stomach. Dinner was still hours away, but she didn't have the energy to seek out a snack to tide her over.

Soaking away the effects of the long drive in the scented bath, Natalie knew she had to make a decision of sorts. Pride demanded it, self-esteem depended upon it.

Alex had followed her to Edinburgh with the sole purpose of proving she was somehow cheating. Not because he wanted to be with her. Not because he was falling in love, as Natalie had foolishly hoped. But because he thought she was cheating and wanted to prove it.

He had his proof, or thought he did.

Her problem was what to do if he followed her again. She didn't doubt that he would, mainly because he would feel the need to apologize. Natalie knew him well enough to anticipate that his sense of honor would demand it. He would apologize because he had been wrong.

Perhaps he would want to resume the physical relationship they'd begun last night.

That scared Natalie.

She loved him, wanted him. The thought of living without him was devastating.

But he didn't love her. And without even the remotest possibility of changing that, she couldn't bear to see him again.

Not just because he didn't love her. But because she still loved him, and was terrified he might find out.

Pride and self-esteem were all she had.

THE TELEPHONE RANG as she was stepping from the bath.

Natalie wasn't as surprised as she might have been a few days earlier. Although she hadn't told anyone where she was staying, it would have been child's play for Liz to figure it out, and almost as easy for Stanhope. Alex, too, would have concluded she was in the

Lake District, but narrowing it down to Grasmere would take some doing. Natalie placed her bet on Liz.

She was right.

"Stanhope called here yesterday. That man gives me the creeps," Liz said, managing to inflect just enough disgust into her voice to give Natalie goose bumps. "He was practically hysterical when he couldn't find you at the hotel in Edinburgh."

"I got the same impression. He called me in the middle of the night, just to tell me about it."

"What was his problem?"

"I'm not really sure," Natalie answered, wishing she could put her finger on what was bothering her. While he'd been a royal pain the night before, this morning he had been extremely pleasant. "But if he calls me again in the middle of the night, I think I'll quit."

"Good idea," Liz agreed. "Do you want me to tell him?"

Natalie smiled at the offer, amused at her friend's willingness to intercede. But she declined, reserving the privilege for herself. She didn't want to be responsible for another mood swing. He might get hysterical again, and Natalie didn't think she wanted to deal with that. "That's okay, Liz. Just make sure you don't let me in for any more surprises. If he calls, tell him you don't know where I am."

"In other words, lie."

"I prefer to think you're protecting the interests of your employer."

"Gotcha," she replied. "Fib."

"If it works, use it."

"Mrs. Wilkins hasn't called in days," Liz offered. "I think she lost the purple watch and doesn't want me to find it."

"There's always that possibility," Natalie agreed. "But you might check with her, just in case. She gets lonely in that big house, all by herself."

Saying goodbye, Natalie walked over to her suitcase, where she dug around until she found a pair of socks. Pulling them onto her cold toes, she padded to the bed and pulled down the covers. It was odd that Liz hadn't asked about Alex, she thought, as she slipped off her robe and collapsed onto the mattress. Staring at the antique light fixture above her bed, Natalie wondered about that for the longest time.

A POUNDING NOISE penetrated her dream. Like drums, only what were drums doing on the battlements of King Ludwig's castle? And why were the drummers dressed in college gowns and wearing little white caps with ribbons hanging from each side?

Ignoring the drums and the pounding, Natalie snuggled deeper into the blankets, determined to return to the party where everyone was watching an airplane fly loops through the stars.

But the drums intruded again, now thumping in a persistent beat as the drummers circled the round table. Natalie grinned at them, noticing for the first time that a rabbit was in charge of the snare drum and that a mouse was playing the cymbals. This was a lovely party, she thought, eyeing the great mounds of food that covered every inch of the table and licking her lips in anticipation.

Suddenly aware that her stomach was rumbling, Natalie awoke knowing her appetite was out of control.

She also realized someone was pounding on the door.

Even before she opened the door, she knew who was standing on the other side. She could even guess what he was going to say.

Just as Alex brought his hand down to bang on the door, Natalie swung it open. He hit her on the forehead.

"Ouch!" Jumping back into the room, she pressed one palm to her head and the other to her mouth to stop the words that would have appalled her mother. But when the door slammed shut, she remembered it didn't matter and let them flow.

Alex deserved to hear every four-letter word she knew.

"Natalie!"

"Who, me? No, I'm the door. Natalie went to dinner." Turning her back on Alex, she bolted for the bathroom. Not because she was really hurt, but because she was in a bedroom with Alex and wasn't even dressed. Naked under the light, silk robe, she felt threatened. Vulnerable. And very, very afraid—not of Alex, but of herself.

"Quit joking around and let me see!" he demanded, shooting out a hand to snag her wrist and draw her closer. He reached up to remove her hand from her forehead. One by one, he gently pried her fingers away until he could see the wound, then he lifted his hand again to brush away the wisps of hair at her temple.

Natalie didn't move a muscle and very nearly quit breathing. Standing this close couldn't be good for her, she thought, no matter how good it felt. Touching him was wrong, especially when she was angry and hurt and miserable. She shouldn't have let it happen, but how could she change things?

She couldn't, because he didn't love her.

Pride. Self-esteem. Respect.

"Let go of me!" she pleaded, trying very hard to make it sound like a command. The light caress of healing fingers on her forehead had startled her, revealing how vulnerable she was, his long, hard body somehow managing to warm her, though they were not touching.

"I didn't want to hurt you," he said quietly, and she knew he wasn't talking about the wound. Then he dipped his head to slide his lips across her brow, and Natalie struggled to ignore the flare of excitement that ignited deep inside her. He winced when he touched the lump that was beginning to form; he suddenly lifted his head and drew away, his expression unbearably grim.

Natalie shut her eyes in frustration, her body cold again, almost trembling from his kiss. *She couldn't let him know. She couldn't ever let him know how much she loved him.*

Carefully maintaining a blank expression, she folded her arms in the classic, defensive position and asked, "How did you find me this time?"

Moving away to lean against the wall beside the large bay window, he appeared unruffled after his dramatic entrance. "Your secretary. She's . . ."

"Entirely too helpful," Natalie finished without giving him a chance. It was her fault. She should have included Alex in her instructions to Liz. But then, she hadn't imagined Liz would dream of handing out her location to just anybody who wanted it!

"Shall I ring for a doctor?" he asked, extracting a pack of cigarettes and a lighter from his breast pocket. But he didn't light one until he'd asked permission, Natalie nodding bemusedly to the silent query of his raised brows.

"I didn't know you smoked."

"I don't," he murmured dryly as he touched a flame to the end of the cigarette.

"What else don't you do?" she asked. Drawing the sash of the robe more tightly around her waist, she moved a few feet away.

But the movement caught and held his attention. Alex sucked in a breath, holding it as he studied the sensuous picture she unwittingly presented. With her hair still mussed from sleep and the robe hugging every curve, she was a temptation he found hard to ignore. Sliding his gaze up and down her body, he found himself remembering in vivid detail everything they'd done the night before, recalling her soft moans of joy, her uninhibited response to his every caress. And he remembered the feel of her soft hands on his own body, at first tentative, finally daring to touch him as he had touched her, her almost uncanny ability to drive him to a level of passion and pleasure he'd never experienced before.

"You don't what?" she prodded. "Besides smoke, that is," she gently teased, staring at the cigarette he held carelessly in one hand. She concentrated on the curl of smoke, not daring to meet his gaze.

"I don't go around hitting women," he said levelly, holding her gaze with his own. "And I don't accuse people of things when they're not guilty." Stabbing out the cigarette in the glass ashtray, he coughed as if something was bothering his throat, then continued. "At least, I never did before."

"It wasn't your fault. At the door, I mean," she said quietly.

She watched as he looked out the window, knowing he was finding this almost as hard as she was. Then his eyes returned to her face and he repeated his earlier question. "Do you want me to ring the doctor?"

"It'll go down by morning," she said, lifting her fingers to explore the bump. Stifling a wince she added, "Don't worry about it." Once he finished what he'd come to say, he could leave.

"I was wrong last night."

"I know." She let him get it out, knowing he wouldn't leave until he did.

"I jumped to conclusions. I should have known better." Could he risk telling her he'd been contemplating love and marriage and children when the telephone rang? That he had just discovered he loved her beyond life itself, and that, in the moments she had been speaking with Stanhope, he had watched his life crumbling into a desolate ruin?

No. Not yet. One thing at a time.

"I didn't telephone New York. I didn't have to," he said, knowing his own sleepless night had matched hers. He knew that because he had watched her all night from the balcony. "After I calmed down, I remembered what you said. And I knew you wouldn't lie. I wanted to tell you last night, but I thought you would be sleeping." He fibbed a little, not wanting her to know he had practically been looking over her shoulder, all but cheering when she found the picture of the candelabra, silently groaning as she checked each and every rope in the room in search of the one in the puzzle.

"Thank you."

"Is that all?" he asked quietly.

"Yes."

"You might take your turn yelling at me," he suggested with the hint of a smile. "It would help.

She shook her head. "It won't." It was too late.

But it wasn't too late to lift her spirits, just a little. At the very least, Natalie realized they could part friends. Putting on the beginnings of a smile, she yielded to the need to give him that much. Friendship. What could be the harm in that?

11

"JUST FRIENDS?" he asked, his dark eyebrows slanting into a frown.

"Yes," she insisted. "Just friends." That was all she could handle, Natalie thought, all she could give him and still maintain her self-esteem. After all the terrible things he had believed . . . she couldn't give him more.

"Friends," she repeated. "Nothing more." Then, because he looked as if he was going to argue, she added, "You followed me all over the place just to prove a point, to prove I was somehow cheating. Not because you wanted to . . . wanted to be with me."

"You're wrong."

"No, I'm not. The proof was in your own words. It's why you jumped to conclusions last night."

Alex stared out the window at the shadows in the garden. Friends, she said. But she had given him more. She had told him *why* she was so hurt. She believed he'd followed her for all the wrong reasons. All he had to do now was convince her that this time, *she* was wrong.

All he had to do. Sighing deeply at the challenge he couldn't turn down, Alex hoped his love for Natalie was strong enough to help him do the job. He had no proof that he was with her because he wanted to be, nothing concrete that would persuade her he only wanted to share his love, his life with her.

But he had a chance, because she had offered him friendship.

Returning his full attention to the woman waiting patiently beside the bed, he nodded without smiling. "Friends, Natalie. Thank you."

Natalie smothered a sigh of relief. But her stomach chose that moment to rumble, loudly enough to draw a startled smile from Alex. "Hungry, Nat?"

"A *real* gentleman wouldn't have said anything," she stated primly, acutely embarrassed.

He nodded in agreement. "A *real* gentleman wouldn't have noticed," he said with a full-sized grin. "Particularly when the woman in question was ... undressed." He had wanted to say it was indecent how the gown clung to her hips and breasts! It was driving him wild.

"Will you have dinner with me?"

"No, thank you." She couldn't do that and keep up the pretense that friendship was all she needed from him.

"A drink then, before dinner?" he persisted. He planned to keep asking until she gave in.

But Natalie couldn't even speak, didn't trust herself to do more than shake her head and stare over his shoulder, into the dark night. There was a long silence before she heard him move. Her breath caught in her chest when he came to stand near her, and she found herself incapable of avoiding his gaze.

"Don't think this is the end of it, Natalie," he murmured, one finger reaching out to trace the curve of her brow. "I'll be watching you."

"Why?" she couldn't help asking. But it was hard to concentrate with his finger testing the vulnerable hollow behind her ear.

"Think about it, Natalie," he said, his voice husky with promise. "Just think about it."

Before she could ask again, he dropped his hand and kissed her briefly on the temple. "Good night, love," he whispered. "Enjoy your dinner."

I'LL BE WATCHING YOU, he'd said. *Think about it.*

Natalie did very little else during dinner.

Good night, love. What the hell had he meant by that! Digging into the tender roast beef with a ferocity that brought a waiter scurrying to ask if the meat was perhaps a little tough, she fought back the urge to leave her meal half-eaten and find Alex.

But she didn't know where he'd gone. He wasn't in the hotel. She had checked that first, before she had even dressed for dinner. But it shouldn't matter. He was a friend, no more, she tried to convince herself.

So why couldn't she think of anything else? *Good night, love.* Natalie slammed down her fork, giving the waiter something new to worry about. As he disappeared with the remains of her meal, Natalie mentally counted to ten and swallowed deeply. She would not allow Alex to interfere...not with the puzzle, not with her life!

By the time the waiter returned with the sweet trolley, Natalie found herself greedily selecting one of the more calorie-laden desserts. Sinking her spoon into the heavy cream covering the chocolate cake, her spirits rose.

There was excitement now. Anticipation.

But no reason for either! she reprimanded herself, blaming the euphoria on a sugar high. Alex was her friend. Nothing more, nothing less.

FROM HIS VANTAGE POINT in the gazebo, Ned Murdoch watched and waited until she returned from dinner, relieved to see she was alone.

Alone she was an easy target.

Stanhope had called before dawn, dragging him from a troubled sleep about this woman. Scaring her hadn't worked. Stanhope wanted her dead.

But Murdoch wasn't ready, not yet. He wouldn't have any fun if he just killed her now. He wanted her to know the terror of being followed...hunted. Then, when she knew, killing her would be a release, for both of them.

Hiding behind his newly shaved chin in a dark corner, he'd watched her that night in the dining room. She ignored all the men, even the young hotel manager who had offered to buy her an after-dinner drink.

She ignored them the same way he'd watched his wife ignoring other men. Except with his wife, she'd known when he was watching . . . and when he wasn't.

Natalie Tracy ignored him.

Not at all like how she treated Garrick, of course. He'd seen him touch her. It wasn't so much that he would touch her, but that she would let him. It was a familiar touch, as if they thought they were getting away with something.

Checking the light in her room one last time before leaving, he pictured Natalie Tracy just a little terrified. And smiled.

ALEX WAS GIVING HER some room to breathe. Not much, because he was in the hotel just down the road, but enough.

She was solving the puzzle much faster than he had expected. Her extraordinary ability to decipher the clues now led him to believe she would finish the preliminary steps in record time. Of course, Dempsey Press was giving her some sort of guidance. But if he was correct, it was only a timesaving device and not an attempt to breach the integrity of the puzzle.

Now he was concerned that Natalie would reach the end with enough time to discover it was...missing. The Oracle was incomplete, so Natalie didn't have a chance in hell of making the final connection.

But he could worry about that later. Now there were more important matters. Showing Natalie he loved her was one. Making her love him was another.

NATALIE LEFT the surveyor's office in midafternoon. This time she had been investigating the drawing of a mountain, a river and another mountain.

Sighing with resignation, Natalie tentatively admitted she might be pursuing the wrong lead. After a late-night's study of all the clues, she had risen early and arrived at the surveyor's office promptly at nine. But searching the endless stacks of topographical maps for anything that even remotely resembled the drawing had been a losing proposition. She had wasted nearly a whole day.

But she was philosophical about the temporary lack of progress and grateful for the extra time she'd gained in Oxford and Edinburgh. Strolling along the sidewalk, she found herself wondering where Alex might be.

It had been like that all day. Working and wondering, feeling almost as if she could reach out and touch him. It was as if the joke was on her, she mused, stopping to peer into a gallery window before being lured away by the aroma of freshly baked bread. The bakery next door offered such a wide selection that Natalie couldn't resist ordering several of the rich pastries.

She carried her booty across the street into a small park, where she sat down to enjoy her treat on a wooden bench. And again she found herself thinking about Alex.

He was just her friend. And according to her new ground rules, she must not think of him as anything more.

Why? Because he had believed the worst. Because he had *wanted* to believe it.

Are you sure? Natalie didn't immediately jump in with an answer. She didn't have one. She had forgiven him last night—enough to accept him as a friend, but not as a lover. Yes, Alex was her friend now, even though his unexpected remarks had tempted her to believe he wanted more . . . that perhaps he was capable of more.

Crossing her legs on the bench, Indian style, Natalie studied the idea that had been niggling at her since Alex had walked out of her bedroom. He had jumped to the conclusion that Stanhope and she were cheating, yet had admitted the mistake.

Then she had assumed Alex had followed her to prove her involvement with Stanhope. *But what if she was wrong . . . just as Alex had been wrong?*

Natalie stared blankly at the half-eaten apple turnover in her hand, then dumped it back into the sack.

If you can forgive a friend, why not a lover?

"Because he hurt me!" she argued aloud, then had to blush as a couple of passing children shot her worried glances before dashing off. She felt silly, knowing the children probably believed she belonged in the nearest loony bin.

She felt ashamed. She was just as guilty of jumping to conclusions as Alex. Natalie crossed the pavement to toss the unfinished bag of goodies into the garbage can. Her appetite was gone.

What worried her more, Alex was gone. She hadn't seen him all day. Could she afford to take the time to look for him? Probably not, she decided. But she would do it, anyway. Suddenly Alex was more important than the puzzle . . . more important than anything else.

Setting off in the direction of her hotel, so she could dump the heavy research materials in her room, Natalie tried to work out the words that would tell him how sorry she was.

"I'm sorry." That seemed to be the best, so she practiced it, letting it roll softly off her lips as she walked along. She ignored the startled glances of the people she passed, intent upon rehearsing. Natalie didn't bother about what she might say after that. Remembering how she was when Alex was around, she would be lucky to string two words together, so she planned to keep it simple.

"I'm sorry," she repeated, growing more confident with each repetition.

What if it was too late? Natalie stopped abruptly. The man behind her couldn't avoid the collision, but he was tall enough, strong enough and sufficiently in control to keep them from pitching to the hard concrete.

Natalie said the first thing that came into her head. "I'm sorry!"

"I know."

"It's you!"

Alex just smiled as he guided her out of the center of the walk, where they were attracting interested glances, and over to a shop window that was curiously devoid of gawking tourists. Natalie glanced inside and was rewarded by a lavish display of turkeys, hanging by the neck with feathers intact. A butcher shop, she realized. How romantic!

But she had something else to say. "I'm sorry." There! That was out of the way.

"You've already said that once," he pointed out, drawing her aside so she didn't have to look at all the dead turkeys. Placing her with her back to the wall, he stood over her, drawing a shield of privacy around them as he leaned his forearm on the wall near her head.

"But that was when I thought you were a stranger crashing into me," she explained. "The second one was for you."

Alex grinned. "What about all the other ones you scattered along the way?"

"That was practice."

"Why?"

"Why did I practice?"

"No, why are you sorry?"

"Because I jumped to a wrong conclusion just like you did, and didn't have the brains to know it. So I needed to apologize." Taking a swift breath, she asked before she lost her nerve, "Was it really a wrong conclusion?"

Her heart almost stopped in the time he took to answer.

"I followed you because I wanted to be near you."

"Why?"

"Why what?"

"Why do you want . . . ?" But she couldn't finish, because the teasing grin on his face made her catch her breath. She felt a blush cover her face.

"Will you have dinner with me tonight?"

"When?"

"Sometime appropriate, say... at dinnertime?"

"Oh." Natalie was disappointed. She wanted to spend the rest of the afternoon with him, couldn't understand why he was putting her off until later.

"I think you have work to do," Alex reminded her gently.

"I could probably accomplish something or other," she admitted grudgingly.

"And I have a few calls to make." There were other things to do, too, like finding the best, most intimate restaurant in the area and booking a table. Things like finding a florist and choosing some flowers.

Things like planning an evening they would never forget.

Natalie was disappointed, but tried to be brave. "Does this mean I have to spend the rest of this beautiful afternoon in the surveyor's office?"

"If that gets the job done, then yes."

But he didn't hint one way or the other whether it would get the job done, and Natalie grinned in response to Alex's broad smile.

Conscious of the never-ending flow of people around them, Alex didn't even consider kissing Natalie. One kiss wouldn't be enough, and a peck on the cheek was more temptation than he could stand. So he straightened from the wall and pushed Natalie away before he could change his mind. "Go to work!" he shouted after her. "I'll see you at seven."

Natalie tried not to trip as she moved along, walking backward so she could watch Alex before he melted into the distance. But she backed into an ice-cream trolley, and by the time she'd sorted out both herself and the excited vendor, Alex was gone.

All the same, he'd be back! Whistling an off-key version of "Happy Days Are Here Again," Natalie headed back to the dingy office on the outskirts.

The driver of the dark sedan winced when she stepped off the curb without looking. Three seconds and she could be dead. Instead, he gripped the wheel and watched her pass through the office door across the road. It was a shame he had to pass up such a perfect opportunity.

But he consoled himself with the assurance that there would be others. From what Stanhope had said about the treasure hunt, the Tracy woman would have to take a long walk over the hills—fells, they called them up here—to solve this part of the puzzle.

He grinned widely, then pulled away. It would take all night to drive home and back, but it couldn't be helped. The rifle he stored beneath the floorboards of his kitchen couldn't have been carried on the train.

Reminding himself to call Stanhope from home, he turned right as he left the village and headed south.

It was going to be a long night.

"I'VE BEEN CHASING a dead end, I think." Natalie tried to mask her impatience. "But I'm ahead of schedule, so there's nothing to worry about." At least she had returned to the hotel with a new idea. But since she could do nothing until the next morning, she decided to put the puzzle out of her mind.

There were better ways to spend her evening than talking to Stanhope.

"Probably not," he assured her. "Call tomorrow and let me know how things stand."

Instead of answering, Natalie made a strangling noise and rubbed her sleeve over the instrument in an attempt to simulate interference.

"Natalie?"

"Can't hear you, Neil," she whispered just loudly enough to get her message across. "Connection's gone . . . can't . . . talk . . . soon." And she gently replaced the receiver before he could argue, still disgusted with his slimy insistence that she call him Neil. Yuck!

Attributing her overreaction to extreme dislike, Natalie immediately forgot Stanhope and concentrated on the night to come. Checking her watch, she found she had just enough time to call Liz before Alex arrived.

Liz was due for a reprimand for giving her address to anyone who called. And when she'd finished with that, she'd give her a bonus, because without Liz's interference, Alex would never have found her.

The phone rang before she could lift it.

"I've got bad news." Alex's voice sent a thrill down her spine.

"How bad?"

"I have to return home. Now. There are some problems, and I need to be there."

Natalie couldn't keep the disappointment out of her voice. "When do you have to go?"

"I'm on my way now." Then he paused, as if he couldn't decide what to say. "Sorry about dinner."

The hell with dinner. It was Alex she needed, not food. "When will . . . ?"

"As soon as I can, love. As soon as I can."

"Is there anything I can do to help?" With whatever, she finished, silently urging him to share his problems.

"No. Not now. I have to take care of it myself."

Natalie made up her mind to be brave. "Call me?"

"Of course." And then, as if to reassure her, he rattled off his telephone number. "You can leave a message there anytime, love."

Twice. He'd said "love" twice. Her heart had done somersaults both times. "Goodbye, Alex. Take care." Before she could change her mind and blurt out how much she'd miss him, how much she loved him and everything else she wanted to say, Natalie cradled the receiver.

When he returned she would tell him. Not over the telephone, but face-to-face.

She owed him that.

ALEX STARED at the buzzing instrument before he finally returned it to the table. She had hung up on him, more or less.

But she hadn't protested when he called her "love." Perhaps she hadn't heard?

No. She'd heard. And she'd asked him to phone.

Alex quickly left the room, his spirits restored as he remembered her sweet voice. *Call me?* Yes, he'd call. Every night, until he got things sorted out and could return to her.

In the meantime, his thoughts returned to the problem taking him away from Natalie. Settling behind the wheel of the sports car he'd hired, Alex pulled out of the parking lot and drove carefully through the narrow streets of Grasmere until he reached the main road. It would take him another hour to reach the motorway, but once he got onto it, he would really make good time.

That would land him at home around ten or so, but the people he needed to see would still be up. They had big problems and he had the solution.

Almost a year ago, when his cousin had tried to talk him into composing a puzzle book, the idea hadn't appealed. He enjoyed writing fiction, and was working on the plot of another thriller.

Then, one night at the pub, he'd discovered a reason to raise money, a lot of it, and in a relatively short time.

The education authority was threatening to close the village school for lack of funds. If it closed, the children would then be bussed to other towns, some nearby, others farther away.

The only way to keep the school open was to buy it. That was what Alex was trying to do, without letting anyone know. He had the money—the royalties from his novels and his family's money meant he could easily spare the amount needed for the school. But being an anonymous donor was the tricky part, as both his accountant and solicitor lived in the village. Irrespective of oaths of secrecy, Alex didn't think for a minute that they would keep the identity of the school's savior quiet: Being the principal contributor to the school fund would set him apart. The thought of having a few hundred grateful people surrounding him was totally repugnant.

That's where the treasure book came in. He'd sold it to Dempsey Press in New York, under a pen name with the agreement his real name would never be revealed. The royalties were to be handled through a London firm so that not a hint of it would reach Foxfoot.

If everything had gone according to plan, the royalties would have substantially swelled the school fund. Because of Natalie's intervention and because she would not be able to find the treasure—despite how well she was doing—his plan had collapsed.

And time had abruptly run out. The education authority was closing the school nearly a year before the original deadline. As a member of the committee that had been organized to solve this seemingly insoluble problem, he'd been notified that afternoon of the impending crisis.

Smoothly shifting the powerful car into a higher gear, Alex thought about what he was going to say to the men who were waiting for him in Foxfoot.

Then he knew. He would use his own money—openly—and tell them it was being donated by his father. It was brilliant!

Searching for flaws, he saw none. His father could deny the role of benefactor until he was purple in the face—no one would believe him. Alex would see to that. And it would serve the old man right for setting up that trust fund for an unborn grandchild.

Alex smiled, relaxing against the contoured seat as he minutely increased his speed, wondering if his father would think he'd won when he introduced him to Natalie.

Now that the senior Garrick male was donating the needed money for the school, it seemed everyone was getting what they wanted out of the deal. The school got their money, Alex got the girl and, with a little cooperation on Natalie's part, his father got a grandchild.

Wishing Natalie's search for the treasure would end so he could clutter her mind with words of love and marriage, he pulled his attention back to the road in anticipation of an early return to the woman he loved.

12

THE FIRST RICOCHET got her attention. The second one sent her diving behind the nearest boulder.

Murdoch lowered the sights of his gun, then flipped the safety catch before he took a step. Walking around with a loaded rifle was dangerous business, and he was always careful to obey the rules.

He hadn't hit her. He hadn't wanted to. That might have scared her away altogether. Besides, with the silencer at the end of the heavy rifle, it had been hard enough just to bring the rounds close enough to scare her. He couldn't count on not blowing a hole in an arm or leg, or even killing her.

He was tempted to go check behind the boulder and see if she'd fainted, but decided not to risk it. She might just be hiding from him, and he wasn't ready to let her see him yet.

With a sigh of regret he turned back into the trees. He would wait in his car. From there he could watch when she came down the hill, might even see traces of fear in her movements. Knowing she was afraid would be enough for now.

IT WAS NEARLY DARK when Natalie finally awoke.

She knew immediately where she was. Up a hill, behind a boulder, over a cliff, on a ledge.

It sounded so natural when she listened to it in her head. Dragging herself into a sitting position, she winced as the cutting edges of loose rock bit into her bruised backside. But that was something she could handle, and she carefully cleared the rubble from a small spot and tried sitting up again. This time she was successful, and her spirits lifted.

The little things were more than enough to occupy her thoughts at the moment. Knowing where she was and what had happened was enough to boggle the mind, and she needed to take things slowly.

Otherwise she could easily imagine giving in to the panic that was just around the corner. Or over the ledge. Refusing to even look toward the precipice, Natalie tried not to imagine the thousands of miles she would fall if she went over. But that was looking on the negative side, she scolded herself, because it was likely only fifty feet or so—far enough to kill her, but short enough to make sure she didn't have time to worry about it on the way down.

Panic edged in from her blind side, and Natalie shook herself out of the defeatist attitude and made an effort to return to the basics.

She had plenty of room to move around. In the waning light she could easily see that her ledge was just a few feet from the top of the mountain. That was the good news.

The bad news was the rapidly encroaching night. Natalie was well aware of the dangers to lost walkers among the hills of the Lake District. The hotel manager had cautioned her against trying to walk alone, but she had been determined. After all, the solution to the puzzle was out here and she had to find it.

She guessed that was part of the good news, because she had found it. Just before that maniac had started taking potshots at her, Natalie had figured out why she'd had to climb the mountain—well, hill. But getting excited about her success would come later. The puzzle was immaterial at the moment. Getting out of here was taking on critical importance. Carefully drawing herself up, Natalie was delighted to find everything still attached and working. Outside of a few bruises and minor scrapes on her hands and face, she was fit and ready to travel.

The climb back up to the boulder didn't worry her too much. It looked simple enough. But the coming night, combined with the possibility that *he* was still out there, made her reconsider her options.

There were none. She had to get out before it was too dark to see. Reaching up to grab a small tree, she gingerly climbed the few feet of rock. Fortunately the grassy slope wasn't far away, and with a cautious, slithering movement that kept her close to the ground and away from the gaping void at her back, she dragged herself forward.

Once she hit the slope, it was easier. But Natalie didn't let herself get too complacent, not until she reached the boulder and wrapped her arms around its bulk.

Now that the worst was over, she let herself panic. Not a lot, because there was still a black mountain to negotiate . . . not to mention the maniac. But the solid void of blackness frightened her more.

"Hoot, hoot." The innocent noise stopped her in her tracks. With her thoughts on the crazy guy behind the gun, the owl nearly frightened her to death. Her heart stopped, her knees turned to rubber, and she sank into the soft grass at her feet. She could only be brave in doses and had momentarily come to the end of her courage.

She was cold and tired and bruised. While her sheepskin coat had been more than adequate protection from the afternoon winds and might even have cushioned her fall, it couldn't stop the tremors that shook her now. She was frightened and alone.

Shot at by someone she hadn't even seen, almost falling to her death and then terrorized by a noisy owl ... That brought an involuntary grin, and she was suddenly back in control. Terrorized by an owl! What would Alex say?

Standing up and meticulously brushing away the bits of grass and dirt that clung to her jeans, Natalie immediately noticed a change in her surroundings. Just minutes ago, after she'd scaled the cliff—the slight exaggeration bolstered her confidence—she hadn't been able to see anything at all. Now there was light everywhere. Not artificial, but the most natural light of all. The stars. A shining half moon added to their brilliance.

With the ability to walk came the realization that the maniac was gone. He had to be. Otherwise, why hadn't he taken another shot at her? Grimacing, Natalie realized he had probably climbed the hill to see her unconscious on the ledge.

And had left her for dead.

Taking care not to step on a loose rock, Natalie began the short walk back to the hotel. Why hadn't anyone heard the shots? she wondered. But come to think of it, she hadn't heard them, either. She'd just noticed the ricochets and hadn't stuck around to ask why there was no other noise.

Had anyone from the hotel missed her? They should have, because she hadn't been so foolish as to walk off without telling someone. Then again, it was just a few minutes after dark, and if they wondered where she was, it wouldn't be until dinner.

Taking the long way around a group of boulders, Natalie quit avoiding the primary issue. *Who had shot at her and why?*

Almost being run down by the Land-Rover in the Cotswolds might have been the fault of a careless driver. Losing the brakes in her car near Edinburgh could have happened to anyone. But when someone started shooting at her, Natalie had to face facts.

Finding the downward slope easier to negotiate, she concentrated on listing the suspects. Liz, Stanhope, Alex. They were the only people who knew where she was.

She immediately eliminated Liz. Not even in her most paranoid moments could she believe Liz would do such a thing.

Stanhope? True, he'd been acting rather strangely, but why would he want to hurt her? He was just as anxious as she was about the treasure hunt. And the first two incidents might have slowed her down if she had recognized them as warnings.

But she hadn't, and her progress had been steady. On top of that, Stanhope had been almost excited about the positive results she'd shown the last few days. True, she'd been in the Lake District for four days now, but she was finished and could leave as soon as she called to confirm.

That left Alex.

By the time Natalie reached the main road just a hundred yards down from the hotel, she was having trouble walking. She knew it would be easier if she could see, but the tears forming in her eyes were making it difficult.

Alex was the only one with a motive—even though she didn't understand it. But he had been against the test from the beginning.

And Alex was the only one who was here. With both Liz and Stanhope across the ocean, they made unlikely suspects. But Alex had both opportunity and proximity on his side. Even today she couldn't be sure he was at his home in the Cotswolds.

Pushing at the heavy door of the hotel, Natalie made a dash for the stairs before anyone saw her, and ran straight to her room. Throwing the bolt home behind her, Natalie breathed deeply for the first time since that afternoon. She was finally safe.

"Hello, love."

Natalie turned from the door to see Alex standing in front of the bay window.

He was smiling.

MURDOCH WAITED for what seemed an eternity, but still she didn't come.

He waited until it was too dark to see across the road, waited until the stars began to light the night landscape, and she still didn't come down.

He could wait no longer.

He went after her.

But it wasn't his lucky night. At least a dozen paths led to the top of that hill, and it soon became clear that he'd chosen the wrong one. And while he could see by the light of the stars, he could not see through the boulders, trees and bushes that were scattered across the hillside.

He spent the hours until midnight searching the hillside, until cold, hungry and miserable, he finally returned to his car.

He hoped she was still out there.

Throwing the car into gear, he shot down the road toward the guest house where he was staying. Changing his mind at the last second, he drove right into the parking lot of the woman's hotel. Careful not to slam the car door, he followed the path around the side of the converted mansion until he reached the gazebo.

He had a hunch. He prayed he was wrong.

"I NEVER faint!"

"I never smoke," Alex teased, drawing the wet cloth across her forehead and down the curve of her jaw, probably getting the pillow wet but she didn't care.

"I asked you not to do that," Natalie reminded him, moving her head into the curve of his palm. It felt so good, so warm . . . so right. But then, everything had felt wonderful since she'd woken up to find a soft bed under her bruised body and a warm, concerned Alex anxiously hovering over her. Fainting had its positive side, Natalie decided and snuggled closer to the hard length of thigh beside her.

"This?" he asked innocently, scrubbing lightly at another smudge of dirt on her chin.

"You know perfectly well what I'm talking about!" she insisted, blissfully happy to let Alex wash anything he wanted. "That miserable habit you have of sneaking up on me is what I mean."

"Oh, that habit," he murmured, dipping his head close enough to draw his tongue across the tiny dimple in her cheek. "When are you going to tell me why you're such a mess?" he asked.

Natalie shivered and tried to turn her mouth to meet his. But he lifted his head away, his eyes silently daring her to protest.

So she changed tactics, carefully ignoring the mischievous twist of his lips.

"When are you going to tell me how you got into my room?" She eyed him suspiciously. But her instinct told her Alex had had nothing to do with the attempt on her life. True, he was the only one of the three with both motive and opportunity. True, Natalie had built a convincing case against him on that long walk down the mountain.

But seeing him now, she knew she had been wrong. That was twice she'd misjudged him. Twice she hadn't trusted him.

She wouldn't make that same mistake a third time.

"I got in with a key. It's simply abominable how easily one can reach behind an unguarded reception desk."

"Of course." The easy way was always the best.

"So what have you been doing outside after dark?" he asked again. Natalie started to tell him, but he brushed aside a thick wave of hair and stiffened. "What the hell is this?"

"Let me have a mirror and I'll tell you," she said blandly. Nothing hurt, not even the bruise she knew was forming somewhere in the vicinity of her lower back. Just to have Alex with her, touching her, was enough to take the pain away.

"Don't joke, Nat! There are some bad scrapes here. You're hurt!"

"Not a lot," she said. "It could have been worse." And she told him everything.

"WHY DIDN'T YOU tell me about all of this before?"

"There was no all of this. I didn't know anything was wrong until today." It wasn't easy to sound logical, particularly when she was lying naked beneath a shallow layer of bubbles and Alex wasn't making any pretense of not staring at her.

"Is that the only reason?"

"If you mean did I suspect you, then yes, I did." The hurt glittered in his dark eyes, and she hurried to finish. "But only for a few minutes. I even suspected Liz, and that's crazy!"

Reaching out a sudsy hand to reassure him, she touched his thigh in a light caress. The hurt left his eyes, replaced by the more familiar glint of fiery need. Natalie withdrew her fingers, scalded by the heated contact, but the imprint she made on his slacks left more than a wet mark. It left them both hot and wanting.

"What changed your mind?"

"I decided I had to start trusting you sometime," she replied honestly.

But he was adamant. "You fainted. When you saw I was here, you fainted."

"You scared me!" she exclaimed. "And I was cold and tired and miserable because you weren't here—well, weren't supposed to be here—of course I fainted!"

A spark of indefinable emotion lighted his eyes, making her hope the inquisition was at an end. But he continued.

She let him talk without interruption, mostly ignoring words like, *police*, *protect* and *safety*, letting the husky timbre of his voice lull her into a state of total relaxation instead. Then, after what she figured had to be at least five minutes, she uttered one word. "No."

"No?"

Natalie lifted her lashes in a lazy motion. "No. No, I'm not going to tell the authorities. Even if they believed me, what could they do? No, I'm not going to waste tomorrow trying. And no, I'm not quitting the puzzle, just because some maniac is after me."

Alex glared into emerald eyes that remained inflexibly defiant. But Natalie didn't so much as blink under his fierce stare, and he found himself confronted with the fact that she was determined to do things her way.

He would have to let her. For a while, anyway. But he was going to be at her side. It was a compromise, one she was going to have to live with.

In the meantime, they had better ways to pass the time than arguing. "Have you had enough of that bath yet?" he asked quietly, letting his gaze travel slowly and seductively down her bubble-covered body. Her nipples tightened, then her fingers clenched as his eyes moved lazily onward.

Natalie reflexively pulled up one knee, hiding the dark triangle from his probing gaze. She shivered, although the water was still hot, and waited breathlessly for his eyes to return to her face. It took almost longer than she could bear, but finally Alex showed her eyes that were once again hot with desire.

"Had enough?" he repeated, this time leaning forward to dip a hand into the bath water.

Natalie's reply caught in her throat as skillful fingers curled tightly around first one erect nipple, then the other. But she swallowed hard, forcing an answer. "I, er, could get out," she stuttered, not knowing how she'd find the strength.

She needn't have worried. Alex nodded abruptly, then reached down and lifted her gently against his chest.

"I'll get you wet."

"Nothing can put out this fire, love," he said and kissed her.

Natalie was stunned by the force of her response. An amazing bolt of heat consumed and overwhelmed her and left her trembling in his arms. The hard strength of his lips invaded her soul as he held her in a grip that was every bit as tender as it was insistent. She was helpless to do anything more than follow his lead, sharing his passion even as she wanted more.

He raised his head, with a question in the smoldering depths of his eyes. He wasn't asking if she would make love with him.

He was asking her why she wanted to.

She told him. "Because I love you."

"Good." He didn't say he loved her in return, but she didn't mind that he couldn't say the words. They would come later, she knew, her heart confident as he carried her to the bed. After he got used to the idea.

Bracing his forearms on either side of her head, Alex tried very hard to slow down, to consider the bruised body of the woman who lay damp and waiting beneath him. But when her lips found the pulse at his throat, it was almost more than he could stand.

Nerves tingled everywhere. The sensitive pads of her fingers smoothed again and again over the broad expanse of shoulders that towered above her. But those same shoulders were covered in cloth, and Natalie cried in disappointment when her fingers were unable to master the intricacies of the buttons.

Her cries were smothered as his mouth came down onto hers, wet and seeking as he once again pushed his tongue past her teeth and stroked an erotic message of desire. Her back arched in response to his bold kiss, and her hips encountered the hard proof of his need.

With a groan Alex levered himself away, rising to stand beside the bed as he pulled at the buttons of his shirt. He took pleasure in watching her quivering body, holding her gaze as he unfastened his belt and pushed his slacks down his thighs. Quickly finishing, he stood over her, and his eyes stroked her in a caress that drove her wild with need.

Natalie could feel his gaze on each nipple before it fell to touch the silken triangle of curls. Almost as if her body was reacting to his touch, her legs parted for him. The bold invitation visibly tightened his body, wrenching an almost painful groan from his lips. But when she reached out her arms, begging him to return, he shook his head. She cried out in frustration as she watched him cross to the windows.

Shooting her a quick glance, he quickly drew the curtains against the dark night. "It's your fault, my love. You touch me, and I forget everything."

"You touched me first," she whispered, still breathless and totally aroused; she was past the point where modesty was an issue. "Who is there to notice this late, anyway?"

He shrugged, the slight movement drawing her gaze to his chest. She hadn't had time to really look at him before, she realized, enjoying the way the soft lights cast shadows across the smooth flesh. He was strong. She remembered the feel of hard muscles, knew his strength was just as erotic as his gentleness.

"This way we can leave the lights on. I like to see what I'm touching. It feels . . . different that way," he confided, drawing a single finger along her leg.

Natalie caught her breath, grasping handfuls of the quilt when his finger finally came to rest at the top of her thigh, just a breath away from the part of her that was hot and damp and desperate for his touch. She felt the mattress shift as he lowered himself to sit beside her.

"When I see you, I want you. When I touch you, I know you're mine," he said softly, then bent forward to catch the tip of her breast between his teeth.

"You don't have to touch me to know that," she breathed, each word almost eclipsed by the effort it took to get it out. His hand hadn't moved, and after a gentle caress with his lips, his mouth left her breast.

"It might take a while for me to get used to that," he said, daring her to argue the point.

"I guess I'll just have to be patient...."

Alex smiled, then rested the palm of his hand just below her navel. "I wouldn't want you to get too bored." He rubbed his fingers against her soft skin. "I'll have to vary it, just to keep you interested." Dropping his hand to rest it between her legs, he pressed upward, rotating his palm against her.

She tried to reach out, but he eluded her, moving just beyond her reach without changing the pressure of his hand against the wet heat between her legs. "I want to touch..." she breathed, then was rocked by another tremor as he slid his fingers into her.

"There will be time for that later, love," he said, pretending to soothe her, fondling the nub of her excitement with his thumb as his fingers established a relentless pace. "I want the pleasure of watching you first. If you touch me, you'll deny me that... because I'll be inside you harder and faster than you could ever imagine." Then, through lashes that nearly obscured her view, she saw his expression change to one of curiosity. "Do you like it that way? Hot and fast and hard?" he asked, but didn't give her a chance to answer. "I hope so. We'll probably do that a lot."

"I would like..." she whispered, then a moan escaped her lips as he increased the pressure of his hand.

"I need..." she tried again, but Alex lowered his mouth to her breast, this time drawing her deep into his mouth in a sucking motion that stole any remaining rational thoughts.

"I know what you want, love," he murmured before taking the other breast into his mouth. "You just have to learn to wait for it."

Natalie waited. She had no choice. Thwarting another attempt to draw the length of his body down to hers, Alex held her hands securely away from his own glistening skin and proceeded to drive her to heights she had never before imagined. She thrashed against the power of his lips, rode the magic of his fingers and, finally, could not prevent a startled cry when he allowed her to glimpse the peak.

A heartbeat later he was deep inside her, plunging with a rhythm that arrested her descent and sent her soaring to new heights.

Hot, fast, hard. It was everything he had promised. More exciting than anything she'd ever known, a whole, new world, where love and passion blended into an erotic fantasy... one that was as warm and binding as their love for each other. And he did love her she knew. Everything he did pointed to it.

Forever, the rhythm said. Then Natalie was carried along the crest of their love in a final explosion that left her clinging to Alex, weak and spent and safe in his arms.

Forever, she told herself.

FROM THE GAZEBO, angry eyes pierced the dark night. Murdoch waited long after the curtain had cut off his view; his anger was so strong that he was incapable of moving.

He'd arrived in time to watch the writer strip off his clothes before drawing the curtains and shutting him out. He was outraged that the woman had tricked him, absolutely furious that she was warm and dry in her bed, while he'd been running all over that bloody mountain.

He should have killed her. She was no better than his wife had been, sneaking around behind his back when she thought he wasn't looking.

Throwing a last, disgusted glance at the window, he followed the path around the side of the hotel and left the garden.

Tomorrow, he decided. Tomorrow he would end the waiting.

13

"NO, I'M NOT letting you drive."

"But it'll take hours to get to Cornwall," she protested.

"I'll manage," he said dryly. He didn't want an argument, because that would have been a waste of energy, not to mention self-defeating. Alex didn't have the slightest intention of letting Natalie drive, because he wanted her to rest.

So he let her believe he didn't trust her with his car. It was the coward's way out, but his conscience was clear. The angry bruises on her body were testimony to her ordeal on the mountain the day before, and he wasn't even sure she should be out of bed.

Exaggerating her huffy attitude, Natalie folded her arms and concentrated on the road. The miles were dropping away quickly under the wheels of the luxurious auto, and Alex's superb skill behind the wheel soon relaxed her.

Skill? Alex? Was this the same man who had managed to frighten her nearly half to death during their Cotswold tour? Natalie leaned against the door, studying his calm appearance as he effortlessly guided the Jaguar past an enormous truck. No flash, no excitement. Just a finesse that put him into a category of natural drivers.

"Did you think you could scare me away?" she asked into the near silence of the purring car.

"Excuse me?"

"Your driving," she said, unsure whether she was amused or irritated by his earlier efforts to frighten her out of her wits. "The other day in the Land-Rover. You had trouble keeping the thing on the road, much less headed in the right direction."

"Oh, that."

"Yes, that!"

"I have a tendency to drive all cars like I do the Jaguar," he admitted with a note of chagrin in his voice. "Unfortunately, the Land-Rover doesn't respond as well as I'd like."

"Now that's an understatement." She grinned, thoroughly charmed by the bright red spots of color high on Alex's cheeks. But she made a practical note not to suggest using the Land-Rover again—ever! Chances like that just weren't worth taking.

Then Natalie remembered what she had been thinking about in the shower, before Alex had interrupted her with a very erotic lesson in communal bathing. She shivered in delight, allowing herself to be momentarily sidetracked by the memory before pressing on to more serious matters.

"I think it's Stanhope."

"Why?" It was the obvious conclusion, one he'd reached last night. Alex quirked an eyebrow and waited for her reasons.

"He's the only one besides you and Liz who knew where I was. And since it's not Liz, it must be him."

"And me?" he prodded gently.

But Natalie didn't rise to the bait, contenting herself with a simple, raised eyebrow that produced a chuckle from Alex.

"Anything else?"

"Just that Stanhope's been acting funny through this whole thing," she said.

"Funny how?"

"Funny as in midnight telephone calls," she said, shooting him a look that dared him to comment.

"Go on," he said.

"At the beginning he was fairly stoic and calm about my progress, but then he started to sound...oh, I don't know. Worried, I suppose. Or nervous." Natalie tried to remember the change in Stanhope over the past several days, but it was hard to pinpoint the exact moment when she'd started to get the feeling he was acting oddly. "And when I called him last night, he was, well, bored. It was almost as though he already knew what I was telling him."

Alex thought about it, then phrased his next question very carefully. "How do you think he could know something like that?"

"Well, I was at the memorial when that maniac shot at me," she said, referring to the memorial to a trio of fell walkers who had died in the vicinity. The answer to the puzzle had been in the number of walkers. "If he knew about the puzzle from Stanhope, then it must have been obvious that I had found the answer."

"And reported to Stanhope," Alex finished. It was the same conclusion he'd reached, but hearing it from Natalie confirmed it. "So that leaves us with a man who works for Stanhope."

"Yeah." Natalie shivered, this time out of nervousness. "I'm glad I didn't think about this last night." It had been late when she had remembered to call Stanhope, but not an unreasonable hour in New York. She really hadn't been in the mood to make the call at all, but was determined to leave for Cornwall in the morning. After her narrow escape on the hillside, Natalie had wanted to get as far away from Grasmere as possible.

But now that she realized Stanhope had to be at the bottom of all her trouble, she began to worry. He knew where she was headed next, had probably arranged another accident. An arrow of fear shot down her spine, and Natalie nervously chewed at her lower lip as she considered what that meant.

"He won't even get close," Alex said positively. Reaching out a hand, he took Natalie's quivering palm into his own and soothed her with his confident strength. "He'll have to get you alone before he tries anything, and that just won't happen," he promised.

Natalie believed him because she trusted him. Smiling tentatively, she pursued the other side of the question. "So what is Stanhope afraid I'll find?"

"I'm not sure." Alex had given that some thought, and had a pretty good idea what the problem was. But discussing the treasure beyond very broad generalities was taboo, and he couldn't mention his suspicions without breaking this agreement. "But I think I'll call Brooks in New York and see what I can dig up."

"Why don't you just tell them about Stanhope and get them to take care of him?" she asked.

"Proof," he answered. "We've got suspicions, but no proof. If we go after him now, without evidence, he'll probably get away with it—whatever it is. At the very least he'll have enough warning to get away."

"Dempsey Press gave me an alternate contact, just in case Stanhope wasn't available. I suppose I'll have to start using it."

"I'm not sure you should pursue this at all."

Natalie stiffened, rejecting Alex's words without a second thought. Giving up was not an option she was prepared to consider. "Wrong. I'm going to finish this thing. I'm not working for Stanhope, so there's no reason to quit. They'll just have to get him out of my way."

"You're being unreasonable," he exclaimed. "Stanhope isn't just in your way. He's trying to *kill* you."

"Once we let him know we're on to him, there won't be a problem."

"What about his friend in England, the one who's been following you?" he shot back. "Are you going to reason with him, too? Are you sure he'll stop bothering you, just because you know about him?"

"We'll have to get Stanhope to take care of him."

"That would be the last thing he'd do. Once we confront Stanhope, he'll be too worried about saving his own skin to be concerned about the mess he's got you into over here."

"Then I guess we have a no-win situation here," Natalie concluded, still unwilling to give an inch. "We can't get to Stanhope without proof, and we have to pretend everything is just peachy, because we don't want to let him know we're on to him."

Alex sighed heavily and impatiently dragged a hand through his hair. Natalie was being obstinate, and there didn't seem to be any way of stopping her, apart from locking her up somewhere. The idea had merit, but he knew better than to try it. She would never forgive him.

But that wasn't the reason he wouldn't do it. He could live without forgiveness, especially if it meant she was still alive. No, the main reason was the man with the gun. They had to find him and stop him. If Natalie suddenly disappeared, the man would do the same.

She would never be safe until he was caught.

Alex was working on a plan, but needed to make some phone calls. Then he would tell Natalie about it and to hell with her objection to police involvement. In the meantime he decided to give in. With conditions, of course.

"If you insist upon pursuing *The Quest* it will have to be with me." Holding her startled glance for just a moment, he listed the terms. "I won't leave your side for a minute."

"How am I supposed to concentrate on the puzzle with you hanging all over me?" she asked, skeptical that she could accomplish anything with Alex on her heels.

"Take it or leave it, Nat." His tone brooked no arguments, and he waited patiently for Natalie to accept his terms.

"I'll take it," she said softly, and fell silent.

Alex added a few refinements to his plan, making a mental list of the people he would need to consult. It would be up to Dempsey Press to make contact with the New York police, once they had evidence of Stanhope's complicity. Alex would see to alerting the authorities in Cornwall. He would need their assistance, if the plan was going to work. But that would mean digging up some contacts at Scotland Yard, and getting the word through that he wasn't some joker who was taking them for a ride.

Natalie's thoughts were very different.

She smiled softly, remembering the gentleness with which he had made love to her in the early hours of the morning. They had shared passion. And words of love even though Alex had managed to avoid the three most important ones—I love you. But her smile broadened because she thought it was funny that a man of so many words couldn't say three syllables.

They hadn't talked about the future in terms of commitment and vows and promises. But it didn't matter, because she knew. It was in his eyes every time he looked at her, an oath of love that could never be a product of her imagination.

"When do you have to phone Stanhope again?" Alex asked suddenly, jerking her from her fantasy future back into her present nightmare.

"When I have something to tell him."

"How long will that be?"

"Hard to tell. Maybe tonight, perhaps tomorrow night. It depends on how well I do, once we get to Cornwall." Natalie briefly outlined the limits of her contact with the publisher's representative.

"And there's no reason for him to know where you'll be staying tonight?" he quizzed.

"I've always let him know where I was headed, but only generally. He doesn't have the hotel name and won't until I call him with my progress report," she said, pleased now she'd been stubborn about that point earlier in the week. "He found me at Borthwick Castle through my secretary, Liz. But I've let her know she's not to do that again."

Alex nodded, satisfied. Unless the man in Grasmere had followed them today—and Alex was positive he hadn't, because he'd been on the lookout for him—then no one would know their whereabouts.

"I'm not sure I'll be able to call Stanhope, anyway," Natalie said. "The actress part of me stayed back in Boston."

"I don't believe that for a second!" Alex declared with a laugh, fully aware Natalie could do anything she set her mind to. Remembering the occasions when she'd stretched the truth, he knew she had a talent in that direction. The only reason it hadn't worked on him was because he'd anticipated her strategy.

"Well, maybe we can avoid talking to him at all," she offered, positive she couldn't talk to Stanhope without letting him hear her aversion.

"We'll see. Don't worry about it for now," Alex added, dropping her hand to change gears. The six-lane motorway suddenly narrowed to two, and traffic slowed to a crawl. "I'll try to get some answers tonight. Tomorrow evening, at the latest, we'll have a better idea what's going on here."

"And in the meantime?" she wondered.

"In the meantime you concentrate on the puzzle, and I'll make sure you stay alive to do it. Stanhope and his friend can't possibly find us again until you report."

Picking up speed again once they'd passed the bottleneck, Alex patted the books on the seat between them. They were her reference materials, everything she had about the area they were going to visit. "Don't mind me. Just pretend I'm the chauffeur and not the man you made wild, passionate love to last night."

Natalie blushed at his words, but couldn't help adding, "Twice."

"Twice?"

"Last night. We made love twice."

He nodded, grinning at her correction, but still got in the last shot. "We started late."

Before things could get out of hand, Natalie grabbed the first book from the stack and opened it in her lap. But it was ten minutes before the words began to make sense.

ALEX GOT NO ANSWERS from New York that night. The next morning, Natalie was hard at work.

"Don't you think we should get some breakfast first?" Alex pleaded, astonished when Natalie wanted to leave without even a cup of coffee.

"No time," she replied sternly, dragging him through the hall and down the stairs into the hotel lobby. "They won't be open for breakfast for another hour. We could be in Penzance by then!"

"Why didn't you arrange for early coffee last night?" he growled. Perhaps Natalie didn't notice, but he was just a little bit groggy this morning, and it was mainly her fault—although he wasn't complaining.

Natalie stopped in the center of the lobby and whirled to face him. "Are you always this grouchy in the morning?" she asked suspiciously, hands firmly on hips as she challenged him. He wasn't perfect, she was beginning to discover. Neither was she, but coffee had never been a driving force in her life.

"Only when I'm denied most of my sleep and all of my coffee."

"But normally you're okay if you get coffee?" she prodded.

"Mostly."

"Good." She'd remember that in the future. It would make life much easier. But for now she wasn't about to apologize about the lack of sleep. Between the calls to and from New York and another exciting night in Alex's arms, neither of them had managed more than a few hours of rest. Speaking personally, she hoped to repeat the pattern often—without the phone calls, of course.

This morning, however, she was satisfied that he would revert to normal, once she connected him up to a coffeepot. She turned on her heel and dashed out the front door of the hotel, eager to follow the trail of her first clue.

"So what about the coffee?" he asked, hurrying to keep up with her. He'd begun to hope that she'd relented about making him wait until they reached Penzance.

"We'll stop at the first place that's open," she promised, fully aware that nothing would be open for at least an hour. Either way, she won. Jumping into the passenger side of the car, Natalie waited impatiently for Alex to catch up.

She was anxious to move ahead with the treasure hunt . . . and at the same time filled with dread that she would find something that would require a call to Stanhope. But the activity was distracting, and she thought she'd worry less if she stayed busy.

They drove to Penzance.

"I STILL DON'T SEE why I have to call Stanhope."

"Because we can't depend upon him phoning Liz," Alex returned. Shutting the bedroom door behind him, he crossed to a massive chair near the crackling fire. Natalie was already curled up in the matching chair opposite, and he had to restrain himself from reaching over to pull her into his lap. They had a few details left to discuss, and there was her conversation with Stanhope to rehearse. So Alex ignored his slightly raised pulse, determined to get through this before he gave in to his more basic urges. But the picture she presented with her windswept hair and wide, emerald eyes was too much temptation, so he averted his gaze.

"But what if I get it all wrong?"

"We'll write out a script before you phone," he answered patiently. "And I'll be right there with you, love. All you have to remember is that Stanhope is on the other side of a very large body of water. He can't hurt you. He can't even see you."

Natalie considered his arguments, wishing there were another way. But there wasn't, of course. And she trusted Alex enough to know he wouldn't make her do this if it wasn't absolutely essential to his plan.

She'd been amazed when he first told her. Returning to their hotel after a long day of chasing down clues and charging back and forth all over Penzance, Alex had shut himself away with the telephone. Then, just an hour or so later, he'd shared the plan with her.

She was still amazed and excited by its simplicity. Not because there was any real danger, but because it was like a scene from one of his books. Contrary to the popular tendency to write of bloody shoot-outs in dark alleys, Alex had always tried to exercise a little restraint in his confrontational scenes—at least those where the good guys were in control. He'd told her that in his research he'd discovered that where professionals were on top of the situation, the confrontation was normally quiet and bloodless and usually invisible to the innocent bystander.

Alex had conceived a simple plan to catch the man with the gun.

Natalie saw the logic behind setting a trap. Rather than wonder when the maniac was going to strike next, they would control the situation, invite him to make a move—and stop him before he got too close.

"I shouldn't have tried so hard today," she grumbled. "Then there wouldn't be any excuse to call him." But she'd made progress today and now needed direction. She could either spend the next day traipsing around the moors of Cornwall, looking for ancient monoliths, or go to the Jamaica Inn and work from there. Alex's plan was flexible enough to cover both options, but that wasn't the point. If Stanhope knew where Natalie would be the next day he would pass on the information to his accomplice.

Naturally, Alex already knew what Stanhope's response would be. While the monoliths would indeed play a large part in the solving of the puzzle, it was to the Jamaica Inn that she needed to head next. The pub, made famous by Daphne Du Maurier, had been a stopping-off place for smugglers and pirates and was ideally situated for his plan. Located in an isolated village on the moors, access was limited and easily controlled.

"When I was talking with Brooks, he agreed to extend your time limit a little," Alex offered. "Seems they think you might have been delayed somewhat by Stanhope's interference."

"Kind of them to remember me," she huffed. During the whole of the long telephone conversation, the president hadn't once asked to speak with her. Natalie was beginning to get the impression that the test was no longer high on the priority list.

But Alex just grinned. There was a lot he hadn't told her, mostly because she was still determined to solve the puzzle according to the original ground rules. The conversations he'd had with the authorities and Dempsey Press had almost always revolved around the puzzle, and even the most innocent remark might have influenced Natalie. So Alex had handled all the calls behind the closed door of their bedroom, while Natalie twiddled her thumbs in the outer lounge.

"I doubt that they'll give you more than an extra day or two, though. They're pretty anxious to get on with things, especially with the publicity they'll receive from all this."

"Why should they want to advertise having a would-be killer on the premises?"

"I suppose it's the old assumption that any publicity is better than none at all. And as long as the details are kept vague they'll probably generate a lot of interest in the book."

Natalie slammed shut the book she'd been trying to study, suddenly irritated with everything and everyone. "I'm going to take a bath before dinner."

"Want company?" he asked hopefully.

"No!" But before she could take two steps, Alex had reached out to snag her wrist, effectively halting her flight.

"Anything wrong, love?" he asked, drawing himself up to stand just in her path. He wasn't using force to keep her there, and the fingers that had stopped her were now massaging the soft skin of her wrist. Alex brought his other hand to rest gently at her nape, imprisoning her with a gentle touch that was meant to soothe and comfort.

"Of course not!" she sputtered, then immediately regretted her temper. It certainly wasn't Alex's fault, but her nerves were suddenly at breaking point, and she desperately needed a few moments to put everything into perspective.

"Then why so tense?" he murmured, standing close enough for Natalie to feel the whisper of breath on her forehead as he spoke. "Are you upset about something?"

"I guess it's just reaction," she admitted. "It's finally getting to me. All this talk about police and surveillance and scripts is more than I can take right now." But his fingers were already working their special magic, elevating her pulse and altering her focus. After just a caress or two she lost most of her nervousness and was only thinking about Alex and the feelings he aroused.

"How can I help?" he asked softly, lifting both hands to gently cradle her head. "Would you feel better if I kissed you?" He lowered his lips to her upturned mouth and lightly teased her, nipping playfully with his teeth and drawing wet tracks across her lips with his tongue. He played with her like this for a long time, avoiding the depths of her mouth as he coaxed her into an entirely different frame of mind. And when her soft breathing was coming in irregular pants, he stopped.

"We can go on with this, or you can take your bath."

"Not both?"

"Probably not." He sighed regretfully, landing one last, butterfly kiss on the corner of her mouth. "A bath would relax you, and I've got some work to do before dinner." Ignoring the emerald fire that seemed to burn through to his soul, he stepped out of her path and lightly pushed her in the direction of the bedroom. "Don't take all night, love," he warned. "If I have to come looking for you, we just might miss dinner. And I, for one, am hungry."

Natalie paused but didn't turn. She knew she'd seen a deep, burning desire in his eyes that matched the warm caress of his voice, and didn't think her willpower could resist him. She opened the bedroom door.

Uttering another sigh, Alex settled down to work on the script Natalie would need for her conversation with Stanhope.

"How DO WE KNOW he'll show up?" Natalie nervously pulled at her heavy sweater, knowing the chill that shook her wasn't due to the cold.

"He'll be there," Alex said confidently. "This is the only sure bet they've got, at least for the next day or two." *The Quest* would be sending her all over the moors of Cornwall; the Jamaica Inn was the only logical choice.

"What if he sees you?" she asked, shivering again as the open window let in another gust. It was a cold day, the sharp wind a reminder that winter had yet to disappear entirely. Natalie was sitting in the lounge of the inn, pretending to study the pamphlets and books piled beside her chair.

"He won't see me," Alex assured her. "Not that it matters. Another ten minutes of this, and I'll be frozen and won't be able to move at all. Now stop talking to me. He might come in at any moment." Alex was stationed behind the building, just outside the open window, a few feet behind her.

"I still don't think I'll be able to recognize him," she insisted.

"I think you will. He's obviously followed you all over the place, so you've probably seen him."

"But if I don't?"

"That's what we're hiding for," he said patiently. Besides Alex, there were two police officers disguised as waiters and two others in the kitchen. Men were also positioned along the roads leading to the inn. Anyone approaching would be reported to those waiting inside. Alex's police contacts had proved invaluable and ensured the cooperation of the local constabulary. "Now hush. There's a car pulling into the car park. Just get him talking, nothing else. Whatever happens, don't leave with him. He won't dare to try anything here, not with all these people around."

Natalie sighed at the reminder, wondering whether he'd repeated those words twenty-nine or thirty times that morning. Turning back to her books, she tried not to jump every time someone entered the lounge.

For another thirty minutes Natalie pretended to study, while ordinary tourists gravitated to the roaring fire until they were sufficiently warmed to consider browsing through the souvenir stand in the lobby. Natalie was astonished at how easily she was able to fade into the background, be politely greeted and then ignored by the ever-changing groups of visitors.

"Shut that window, Albert!" a high-pitched, female voice demanded. "I feel a terrible draft."

Natalie jumped, then relaxed until she realized the woman was talking about Alex's window. Closing the book in her lap, Natalie studied the crowd that had entered the room. By their accents and the assortment of designer labels that decorated their clothing, it was a snap to tell they were American. It was also easy to tell which one of them was Albert—he was the one headed toward the window. "I'd prefer it open, if you don't mind," she said with a tight smile.

"But it's absolutely freezing in here," the woman insisted.

"I like it." Natalie hoped the crowd wouldn't turn against her. Seven or eight people were gathered around the fire, now obscuring her view of the doorway.

Albert had paused on his way to the window, easily interpreting the determination in Natalie's voice. Natalie exchanged a long look with the man, then nodded in satisfaction. He understood who was going to get her way. She looked back at the woman with the screechy voice, who was just opening her mouth as if to argue. Natalie spoke to her as Albert retraced his steps.

"You'll find it warmer in the bar," she suggested, coolly ignoring a glare that would have roasted fish. Natalie was not in the mood for a showdown.

"Hmph!" With that pronouncement, the woman turned on her heel and stomped out the door. Albert meekly followed. The others in the group had already left, and Natalie was again alone.

"It's about time they left," a voice said from just beyond her shoulder. "You were right to get rid of them."

Natalie actually felt the blood drain from her face. Her body went quite still; her heart beat with an erratic, frightened rhythm. She couldn't talk, as fear gripped her in a paralyzing hold. But an almost involuntary reaction made her rotate her shoulders, so she could see the man behind her.

"No! Don't turn round. No one can see me from the door. They think you're alone in here. I'd like things to stay that way."

She obeyed. The glimpse she'd had was enough. Careful not to make any sudden movements, she reviewed the occasions when she'd seen him. Alex had been right. The man had been there all along, and she'd probably gotten a glimpse of him a dozen times. But it was the morning she'd left the train that she remembered most clearly. Hiding from Alex, watching the rest of the passengers jump onto the platform, Natalie had seen him then. Short, dark hair, dark eyes. Nothing remarkable about him, no reason for her to remember him. She understood how he'd been able to follow her without her noticing.

Now she was alone with a man who wanted her dead. *Where was Alex?*

Of course, Alex was waiting for proof, Natalie reminded herself. You couldn't put a man into jail for talking to you, and there was nothing else to connect him to the attacks. Squashing her panic, Natalie concentrated on her job.

"Who are you?" she asked, chagrined to hear a nervous break in her voice.

"Come on, girl, you know who I am," he said smoothly. Natalie thought she heard him shuffling closer to the chair, but shut out the sense of alarm it provoked. "You've been pretending to ignore me for days now, but I've had enough. It's time this was over."

Natalie gulped. "I didn't see you come in," she managed.

"I know. I slipped in behind the crowd, while you were arguing with that old cow." He was definitely closer. Natalie could feel the slight give in the chair as he leaned on its back. Clasping her hands, she tried to get the answers Alex was waiting to hear. It was all that kept her sane.

"Why have you been following me?" she asked, then flinched as a hand snaked over the chair back and grabbed a mass of hair. But she didn't cry out, not even when he tightened his hold. He moved then, coming to sit on the arm of the chair as he held her tightly in his grasp. She was a prisoner now. His prisoner.

"You *know* why I've been following you! Don't *pretend* with me! *It's too late for that!*" Jerking her head back against the chair, he brought his face within inches of hers. "If you hadn't teased me, I might have let you go with just a few bruises. Even after Stanhope said I had to kill you, I might have let you live. *But you're no better than she was—and I didn't let her live, either!*"

"I haven't . . ." she cried, but the words were cut off before she could get them out. *What was he talking about?*

"Don't lie! I watched you with him!" he screamed, and Natalie screamed with him.

She screamed again, then cried out in pain, terrified, as the man dragged her out of the chair by her hair. Now she was on her knees on the rug before the fireplace. Then, just as suddenly, she was released. Out of the corner of her eye she saw a couple of officers dragging the struggling man out of the room, leaving her alone and shaking in reaction.

At last Alex's arms were around her, soothing, comforting, and holding her as if he'd never let go. He held her tightly, shielding her from the activity around them. Natalie ignored everything but Alex, trembling in his embrace as she choked back the tears that threatened. His murmured caresses of love finally gave her the strength to find control.

He loved her. She was safe. It was over.

"I'm so sorry, love. So sorry." He said it again and again, whispering the cadence until Natalie could stand no more.

Lifting her face to his, she offered her lips in a gesture that was at once forgiving and entreating. "If I let you say you're sorry, will you promise never to let me go?"

He could only nod, but she took that as a promise and lifted her mouth to him.

A long while later he noticed the room had grown quiet. With a groan of frustration, Alex drew his mouth away, then buried his lips in her hair. He'd almost lost her, and the horror of the last few minutes was too new to dismiss easily. "It's my fault, love. You weren't supposed to get hurt. I thought we'd taken care of every possibility." Shuddering, he rocked her in his arms, taking comfort from her warm, *healthy* response.

Natalie drew back a little and studied his somber face. "It wasn't your fault that he was irrational. You thought he would just talk, that all the other people would keep him from doing anything stupid." Lifting her hand to feel the warmth of his face, she added, "How could we guess he'd be crazy? That he had somehow mixed me up with someone else?" What had happened to that poor woman? Natalie silently wondered.

"I was wrong," he admitted reluctantly.

"We were all wrong," she corrected gently. "And it's over. Really over. So quit kicking yourself."

"Kicking myself?" he asked, backing up an inch or two to stare down at his feet.

But Natalie just grinned. This was normal.

Shaking his head, he turned to the constable who had been trying to get his attention for several minutes. Keeping Natalie firmly in his embrace, he worked out the details of official statements, then led Natalie out to the car.

"They didn't spot him," he said as he put the car into gear and turned out of the car park. "They were looking for a man traveling alone. Apparently he got a lift with a group. He came inside with the crowd unnoticed. It's my fault. I really thought we had taken care of everything."

"I still needed to talk with him, get some proof. Spotting him early wouldn't have helped much."

"How can you dismiss it so easily?" he asked. "I nearly got you killed."

"*You* didn't do anything except draw him into the open," Natalie said firmly. "If it hadn't been for your plan, he would have caught up with me when there was no one to stop him from . . ." She shuddered, knowing she would never be able to completely erase the memory of the man screaming at her, his fingers pulling at her hair. But Natalie was made of stronger stuff, and it was Alex who needed her reassurance now. So she firmly put the awful memory aside and continued. "It's over now. I'm alive, you're alive, everything's okay! I just want to get back to work!"

"Back to work?"

"Yeah," she said. "Work." She took one look at the disappointment on Alex's face and relented. "Tomorrow. They gave me the day off, remember. I can think of several ways to spend it."

Alex grinned. "So can I." Holding her hand gingerly as he shifted gears, he accelerated. The hotel wasn't far away, but Alex was impatient.

Natalie just smiled and wondered if he would stop for lunch.

She doubted it.

14

"I THINK we should turn back."

"You have no sense of adventure!" Natalie scolded Alex. "What's a little fog to a born and bred Englishman?"

"This," he said, indicating the thick, swirling mass of moist air, "is not a little fog. This is a lot of fog, and it's sheer idiocy to be out in it."

Natalie conceded his point. "It wasn't like this when we started out."

"That was hours ago."

"Just this last one, then. Please? We can't be that far from it," she pointed out. Natalie had a strong impulse to slide her hand up his sleeve to the thick curls at his collar, but controlled it. The need to touch and the effort it took not to had been problems all day. Each touch led to another, until the caress stoked the banked fires underneath. And that, unfortunately, was what they had to avoid, because Natalie had work to do.

Sighing heavily, she backed away from Alex, removing herself from temptation.

"In this fog we'll never find anything, unless we trip over it!" But he turned to lead the way up the dirt track, unable to say no to anything Natalie wanted.

They had been chasing around after ancient monoliths all morning. Or rather, Natalie had been charging around various fields and pastures with Alex at her heels. The clue she was seeking had something to do with the stone monuments that dotted the English countryside, specifically those in this remote corner of the country. At the moment they were somewhere in the vicinity of one called Men-an-Tol. In the pictures it appeared somewhat less than substantial, the three principal stones standing only about three feet high, two upright stones flanking a doughnut-shaped one.

Natalie didn't see how they could miss it.

Passing Alex on the track, she forged her way through the clinging mist, watching carefully for the sign that would indicate where they needed to cross the stone wall. Like most of the other monuments they'd examined, this one was located in a pasture that belonged to the farmer who maintained the dirt track. While these fascinating monoliths were noted on most tourist guides, they weren't taken seriously as tourist sights. Sidestepping a pile of cow muck, as Alex called it, Natalie trudged up the path. Perhaps Alex was right and they should turn back. This fog was thick!

Then she saw it, a tiny, white sign. Without waiting for Alex, she clambered over the low, stone wall and dived into the heavy cloud of fog blanketing the pasture.

"Natalie! Wait!" Alex shouted. But she was already gone, swallowed by the mist even as he jumped down from the wall. "Natalie!" Getting separated in the fog was dangerous, but cautioning Natalie was a waste of time. Alex dragged up everything he could remember about the field, then relaxed a little. Unless she climbed out of the pasture, there was nowhere else to go. She might get lost, but only within the confines of the small field.

"I'm just over here, Alex," she chided, her disembodied voice traveling through the wall of mist. "Follow the path. It must lead to Men-an-Tol!"

Natalie giggled, once again thrilled by the hunt. With Alex nearby and the horror of yesterday nothing more than a nasty memory, she was happy. Sidestepping a boggy hole in the path, Natalie called a warning back to Alex and picked her way over a rocky hump. She heard Alex call something to her, but dashed up the path, intending to hide.

"Natalie."

It came out of nowhere, a silken whisper that beckoned to her. She whirled toward the voice, straining to see through the impossibly thick fog. But she could see nothing.

"Natalie, I'm over here."

It came again. Soft, deceptively friendly. And horribly frightening.

It was Stanhope!

"Come to me, Natalie," the voice demanded softly. "I need to talk with you."

A cry escaped her lips, and she heard the soft tread of approaching footsteps. Panic welled in her throat, but she clapped a hand over her mouth before she could cry out again. She had to be quiet! He couldn't see her, but he could hear her!

Just the same, she jumped off the path and ran several yards before stopping. Checking over her shoulder, she could see no one.

Not Stanhope, and unfortunately, not Alex.

Where was Alex?

"Natalie!" It was Stanhope again, but with the distortion of the fog, Natalie couldn't tell if he was ten feet or ten yards away. She turned and ran, sloshing through a shallow pool before she remembered that every sound drew him closer. She stumbled, then righted herself, totally disoriented by now. She was afraid to call out to Alex, frightened that her voice would lead Stanhope to her.

"Natalie!"

It was Alex this time.

"Natalie! Don't talk! You'll lead him to you."

"One could say the same for you, Garrick." Stanhope was close enough to Natalie to scare her witless. "It would be as simple for me to follow your voice." Whipping her head around, Natalie peered into the fog, trying in vain to see where he was. He wasn't there, not yet. Taking a chance that he was directly behind her, Natalie moved silently in the opposite direction. Front and back were now meaningless points of reference. She needed to concentrate on moving toward Alex and away from Stanhope.

"You're not after me, Stanhope. I'm not worried," Alex taunted. He was desperate to keep the man talking, knowing he had to find him before Stanhope found Natalie. Alex moved away so that Stanhope couldn't find him.

"You don't think I'll let you walk away from this, do you?" Stanhope wasn't cautious. That worried Alex and warned him. The man must be armed.

The voice came from somewhere to her left this time, and Natalie took an immediate right turn. She *hated* this fog!

"Probably not," Alex agreed from somewhere behind her. "But then, I'll kill you if you so much as lay a hand on Natalie." It was a promise.

"Maybe I should just forget about the girl and kill you instead." Stanhope was in front of her again, and Natalie almost cried out in frustration as she did an abrupt about-face. Taking care to step on the moss underfoot, Natalie tried very hard to move silently.

"What are you doing here anyway, Stanhope?" Alex prodded. "I thought they were supposed to arrest you yesterday."

Stanhope sniggered; the sound carried well through the dense fog. He was farther behind her, though. She quickened her steps, listening carefully to the ghostly dialogue between the two men.

"They gave it away, Garrick," Stanhope gloated. "They couldn't keep from staring at me, watching me all day long. It wasn't hard to figure out."

"So why come here?" Alex asked. Now Natalie could almost believe the two voices were coming from the same direction.

"Revenge," he growled. "Your girlfriend caused me a lot of grief. She owes me."

Natalie shivered, then caught herself as her foot slipped on a flat, wet rock. Taking her eyes off her feet for the first time in several minutes, she saw the gathering of ancient stones. She had found the monolith, Men-an-Tol.

Although the doughnut-shaped stone offered only marginal protection, Natalie quickly picked her way through the outlying stones and crouched behind it. Hole and all, the alternatives were even less attractive. The voices were drifting in her direction, almost as if the men were on parallel paths.

As if on cue, the fog began to lift!

"I can't understand how you found us today," Alex continued. "Especially in the fog. We were hardly able to find this ourselves."

"It was logical. With the answer here, I knew she'd have to come eventually. And at the rate she's been moving through the puzzle, it had to be today." Natalie placed Stanhope somewhere to the left of center, still advancing on the monolith. "So I've been here since morning, waiting for her to show up. Too bad for you that she didn't come alone."

"In other words, you finally struck lucky." From the direction of his words, Alex couldn't be far away.

"For a change," Stanhope agreed almost pleasantly. "After all the rotten luck I've had the last week, I was due."

"Were you really afraid she'd find the treasure?"

"Not really," Stanhope scoffed, the scorn heavy in his voice. "But there was always a possibility she'd stumble onto the hiding place with all that help I was forced to give her. I just couldn't take that chance."

Suddenly both men emerged from the blanket of fog. In a split second Natalie found herself pinned by Stanhope's searching gaze. She watched in fascination as he raised his right arm. He held a gun and was aiming it at the hole in the stone.

Alex was prepared for Stanhope's move. He'd expected the gun, had anticipated this moment.

Correcting the aim of his own weapon, Alex pulled the trigger.

"YOU DIDN'T have to shoot me!"

Alex was wrapping a length of cloth—torn from his shirt—around the bloody hand. Stanhope had finally stopped screaming.

"I did what was necessary," Alex said succinctly, then stood up and hauled Stanhope after him. "I would have been justified in killing you, but this is ancient, holy ground and I didn't want to pollute it. You're lucky I only hit your hand. Let's go," he commanded, and pushed Stanhope down the almost visible path, catching Natalie's hand on the way.

"How about you, love? Is everything all right now?" he asked, casting her a quick glance before returning his attention to the man walking in front of them.

Natalie smiled broadly. "How could it not be all right?" she asked. "Playing blindman's bluff in the fog does great things for the nervous system. Not only am I all right, I'm terrific!"

"Terrific?" Alex asked, not quite sure an hour with Stanhope was anything to get excited about. "Explain that, if you would."

"#101."

"Aha!"

#101 was the answer to the Cornwall section of the puzzle. Crouched behind the doughnut rock, Natalie had suddenly understood what the monolith clue meant. Upright, slender stone plus doughnut plus upright, slender stone equaled #101.

But she still had a question. "Why did you bring a gun?"

Not taking his eyes off Stanhope, Alex explained. "I rang the police this morning while you were in the shower. They told me he was still at large. It didn't make sense to ignore that."

"So what was he after?" she asked curiously. "Besides revenge, I mean."

"The treasure."

"The treasure?" Waiting patiently for Stanhope and Alex to clear the pasture wall, Natalie finally understood. The treasure was the reason behind everything.

"Yes, the treasure." In a voice designed to reach Stanhope, just a few feet in front of them, Alex added, "Because the treasure isn't there anymore, is it, Stanhope?"

"Not for months. My accomplice, Mr. Murdoch, managed to replace the real one with a fake—before it was hidden away."

"Not very bright, Stanhope. Doing it that way rather limits who can be blamed."

"That was certainly a problem," Stanhope agreed. "I'd hoped to pin it on you instead. But with the test coming out of nowhere, there wasn't time."

"That's not really why you're here."

Stanhope picked up the pace a little, then slowed when Alex grabbed him by the collar.

Alex pursued the matter. "You came to retrieve the treasure. Even though we caught your friend, you thought you could still get away with it because he told you where he hid it."

"Damn right!" Stanhope boasted. "And you'll never get it back now. Not if you turn me in." Straightening his shoulders, he walked taller, as if he had a bargaining tool.

Natalie couldn't help but notice the gloating triumph in his voice. She cringed, but was philosophical about the loss. At least they had their lives.

"Sorry to disillusion you, Stanhope," Alex said evenly. "Your partner also told us."

"I don't believe it!" Stanhope stopped just short of the main road and turned to face Alex's drawn weapon.

"Try it," Alex taunted him, then proceeded to give a detailed description of where the real treasure had been secreted the second time.

Natalie watched the other man crumble. Revenge, if there was such a thing, was revolting.

"SO NOW what?"

Snuggling up closer into Alex's warmth, Natalie repeated the question she'd been avoiding all evening. "What do I do now?"

"Why... you go on, I would think," he said, absently stroking her shoulder. Succumbing to the exhaustion of the day's activities, Alex was only half with her.

"Go on?"

"Of course," he said, then yawned. "I don't see what's changed."

"The treasure, for one thing," she persisted, drawing herself out of his arms. Pulling up the sheet to cover her bare breasts, she continued. "How can I look for a treasure that isn't there?"

"It will be, darling." With another yawn, he reached out a determined arm to circle her waist. "But that's not the point." Stirring himself enough to conduct a semi-coherent discussion, he explained, "After all, it's not the treasure you were commissioned to find."

"No?"

"No." Not finding any resistance to his efforts to pull her closer, he tugged the sheet away from her body and drew her against him. "You were engaged to find where the treasure was hidden. Not the treasure itself."

"Ah! . . ." she replied, nearly lost in the erotic world Alex was creating. "The hiding place. Of course!"

"But tomorrow, love," he cautioned. "You're otherwise engaged tonight." And with that warning he tipped his head until their lips touched. Breathless, he waited.

"Tomorrow," she answered into his mouth.

Epilogue

IT HAD BEEN A STRUGGLE, especially the bit where she'd needed the computer.

But it was nearly over now. All of it . . . the puzzle, the game, the treasure hunt—*The Quest*.

She was just steps away from winning. She could *feel* it!

Natalie checked her watch and decided she had time for coffee. Strolling down the sidewalk, she found a pub that advertised morning coffee and passed into the dim barroom. Taking her coffee to a table near the window, she settled herself for a short wait.

Alex would be there soon. He had promised.

No, she didn't think he'd find her in the pub. But last night, before she left Foxfoot to come to the township of Delfy, he'd said he would be there when she found it.

And, no thanks to Alex, she had done it.

Natalie grinned at Alex's ingenuity as she sipped her coffee. All the little clues that had not seemed to mean anything had turned out to be the most important: the round table from Oxford; the airplane flying loops in Edinburgh; the arena she'd discarded in Cornwall.

The engagement ring from the London page had been among the most difficult clues, mainly because Natalie had spent an incredibly long time believing it was more than it was. In the end, she'd recognized it as Princess Di's engagement ring and dumped it onto the list of red herrings.

Not to mention the circus from Canterbury and finally, the Olympic rings she'd ended up with after the trip to Wales.

Added together, they had finally pointed to one thing. They were all round.

It had taken her two days to pull it all together. What one word pointed to every clue? Natalie had been firmly stumped before realising it was yet another word game.

So she had turned to a computer.

Renting computer time had been easy, especially in Oxford. Finding someone who was willing to run the thing was a little harder, but she'd managed that, too.

Natalie had listed every red herring from every city, and had researched every alternative word for each of the clues. *Olympic rings* could easily have been *rings* or *five Olympic rings*, *London Olympics* or numerous other combinations. Natalie had tried them all, combining them with all the variations of the other clues, testing last- and first-letter combinations.

In the end she had only one answer that made any sense.

Olympic rings
Round table
Arena
Circus
Loop (airplane)
Engagement ring

Taking the first letters of all the clues, she'd arrived at the word *Oracle*.

But what to do then? And what about all those numbers?

Checking her research materials, Natalie discovered that the Oracle of Apollo at Delphi was the most famous.

And there happened to be a village in England named Delfy. Using three sets of the numbers she'd collected, Natalie plotted the longitude and latitude of Delfy to confirm her guess.

But she still had some numbers left over.

Arriving in Delfy this morning, she'd found a village high street, lined with shops and absolutely nothing to tell her where to look next. With today as her last day, Natalie had despaired.

Until just moments ago, when she had stopped a construction worker to ask directions to the library. He didn't know where the library was, but he was building a theater. He'd offered the information gratis, proud of his involvement in the construction project.

The Apollo Theatre.

The street number was her fourth numeral. That piece of information had been harder to locate, but the site manager had called the project manager, and the number was confirmed.

No wonder Alex had said she wouldn't finish! The Apollo wasn't scheduled for completion for months yet, and without that very important clue, the Oracle would lead her nowhere.

Natalie smiled into her empty coffee cup, then put it aside. It was time to finish.

WALKING INTO THE BANK directly opposite The Apollo
Theatre—still under construction—Natalie discarded
the fifth numeral as she saw it corresponded to the street
number of the bank. Presenting herself to the bank
manager, she drew a deep breath, then uttered the
magic words. "#101 3." They were the only figures she
hadn't yet used. And the order was correct. The spell-
ing of Oracle had settled that.

"I beg your pardon?" the man asked curiously. "I
don't think I understand."

She tried again. "Oracle #101 3."

"Bingo." Swinging around, Natalie found Alex behind her, a grin pasted across his face that rivaled any
other congratulations she might have earned. "I should
have known you would find something that wasn't even
there," he said, referring to the theater.

"So what is it?" she asked, breathless with excitement. Taking his hands, she ignored the bank manager
and persisted. "What have I been chasing all this time?"

Drawing a velvet case from behind his back, Alex
flipped open the lid.

A brilliant assortment of sapphires and diamonds
flashed out at her. A necklace, a bracelet and a ring.

Natalie still couldn't breathe. "They're beautiful."
And blue. Somehow she was disappointed. Blue had
never been her color—not that it mattered. These
would never belong to her. They would be claimed by
the person who finally solved the treasure hunt.

She didn't notice the departure of the bank manager. It didn't matter that he took the jewels with him.

All she cared about was Alex. Melting into his arms
as if she'd never belonged anywhere else, she forgot the
jewels and the treasure hunt.

Cradling Natalie in one arm as he dug into his pocket with his free hand, he held her gaze until it was time to divert it.

"Green, I believe, is your color," he murmured. Then he placed an emerald ring on her finger, a ring that rivaled the sapphire she'd seen in the jewel box. "Marry me, Natalie?"

Her heart thudded in her chest. There were three other words she wanted to hear.

"Why?" she asked, her eyes clear and sparkling with mischief.

"Because I love you, of course."

"You've never said that before," she pointed out, rising up to brush his lips with her own because it seemed to be the only way she was going to get a kiss.

"You were too busy with *The Quest*."

"I can run a business and love you at the same time," she said with mock censure.

"Speaking of your business—"

"I was considering opening a branch in Oxford," she said. "Unless you have an urge to relocate to Boston on a permanent basis?"

"You'll live with me in Foxfoot, my love?"

"I imagine that's the best way to keep a marriage together," she kidded. "Any other questions?"

"Are you going to say yes to my proposal?" he murmured, bending over so that his mouth breathed the words into hers. It was a little frustrating, having to ask twice, but he wanted to hear the words.

"You mean, 'yes, I'll marry you,' or 'yes, I'll love you forever?'" she asked, all playfulness aside as she permanently opened her heart to the man who had asked her to share his life.

"Both," he demanded.

"Then yes," she whispered just loudly enough for Alex to hear before her mouth joined with his in a kiss that affirmed forever their promise of love.

History is now twice as exciting, twice as romantic!

Harlequin is proud to announce that, by popular demand, Harlequin Historicals will be increasing from two to four titles per month, starting in February 1991.

Even if you've never read a historical romance before, you will love the great stories you've come to expect from favorite authors like Patricia Potter, Lucy Elliot, Ruth Langan and Heather Graham Pozzessere.

Enter the world of Harlequin Historicals and share the adventures of cowboys and captains, pirates and princes.

*Available wherever
Harlequin books are sold.*

NHS

HARLEQUIN
American Romance®
RELIVE THE MEMORIES....

From New York's immigrant experience to San Francisco's Great Quake of '06. From the western front of World War I to the Roaring Twenties. From the indomitable spirit of the thirties to the home front of the Fabulous Forties to the baby-boom fifties... A CENTURY OF AMERICAN ROMANCE takes you on a nostalgic journey.

From the turn of the century to the dawn of the year 2000, you'll revel in the romance of a time gone by and sneak a peek at romance in an exciting future.

Watch for all the CENTURY OF AMERICAN ROMANCE titles coming to you one per month over the next four months in Harlequin American Romance.

Don't miss a day of A CENTURY OF AMERICAN ROMANCE.

A CENTURY OF
AMERICAN ROMANCE
1960s

The women... the men... the passions... the memories...

Harlequin Intrigue®

REBECCA YORK

Labeled a "true master of intrigue" by *Rave Reviews*, bestselling author Rebecca York makes her Harlequin Intrigue debut with an exciting suspenseful new series.

43 Light St.

It looks like a charming old building near the renovated Baltimore waterfront, but inside 43 Light Street lurks danger . . . and romance.

Let Rebecca York introduce you to:

> *Abby Franklin*—a psychologist who risks everything to save a tough adventurer determined to find the truth about his sister's death. . . .
>
> *Jo O'Malley*—a private detective who finds herself matching wits with a serial killer who makes her his next target. . . .
>
> *Laura Roswell*—a lawyer whose inherited share in a development deal lands her in the middle of a murder. And she's the chief suspect. . . .

These are just a few of the occupants of 43 Light Street you'll meet in Harlequin Intrigue's new ongoing series. Don't miss any of the 43 LIGHT STREET books, beginning with #143 LIFE LINE.

And watch for future LIGHT STREET titles, including #155 SHATTERED VOWS (February 1991) and #167 WHISPERS IN THE NIGHT (August 1991).

HI-143-1

HARLEQUIN Temptation

COMING NEXT MONTH

#329 DOCTOR, DARLING Glenda Sanders
(Spinoff from #257 *Daddy, Darling*)

Dr. Sergei Karol was no mere mortal. He was a
microsurgeon, the man who'd saved Polly Mechler's brother
from a disability injury. And Polly... well, Polly was cute,
and she sold plumbing supplies on TV. The great Dr. Karol
had yet to discover that Polly wasn't adorable just for him.
She was a celebrity—and her fame was about to spread
nationwide....

#330 CHANCE IT Joanna Gilpin

Diane Roberts was selling off her real-estate empire and
setting out for adventure. And adventure beckoned in the
form of dynamic Ira Nicholson. On his yacht they set sail on
a course of sensual exploration—with the strict
understanding that this was a temporary affair. Too late, the
cool-headed businesswoman realized she had badly
miscalculated her own heart.

#331 EASY LOVIN' Candace Schuler

Prim and proper Kate Hightower had never fancied herself
as a runaway bride. Yet here she was, in New Orleans,
thousands of miles away from her fiancé, in very *unsuitable*
company. Jesse de Vallerin oozed with Southern charm and
seemed determined to teach Kate how to "loosen up." Were
her jitters just the prenuptial kind... or the result of Jesse's
easy lovin'?

#332 DIFFERENT WORLDS
Elaine K. Stirling (Book I-Lovers Apart)

Dawn Avery's life was her work in the rain forests of Central
America. Michael Garrett was committed to a career in
Western Canada. Their worlds collided in a brief, passionate
affair in Costa Rica that left them breathless, aching for
more. Fate had brought them together. But could their love
go the distance...?